Jessica
and the
Crocodile Knight

David Osborn

JESSICA AND THE CROCODILE KNIGHT

DRAGON
Granada Publishing

Dragon Books
Granada Publishing Ltd
8 Grafton Street, London W1X 3LA

Published by Dragon Books 1985

Published by Granada Publishing
in hardback 1984

Copyright © David Osborn 1984

ISBN 0-583-30540-7

Printed and bound in Great Britain by
Collins, Glasgow

Set in Baskerville

For Lisa, Sophie and Natasha.
'What did the Crocodile say today?'

1

Jessica wanted to be alone to think and the swamp had seemed the only place. Just the same, she almost wished she had not come there.

First of all, it was forbidden. Here and there where the ground seemed hard and safe, thick grass hid mud banks which could swallow you up in a minute. And in the dark waterways that twisted among the gnarled trunks of cypress and mangrove trees, there were sometimes alligators. Only last year, a little girl her own age had been dragged under by one.

It was a spooky place, too. In spite of the southern heat, Jessica shivered. In dark pools there were sometimes mysterious scary splashes. Spanish moss draped the trees causing deep shadows you couldn't quite see into. And occasionally, some huge bird like a heron would unexpectedly whirr upward.

At the end of the narrow path along which she had come, Jessica could see the fence around cousin Andrew's and cousin Mary Lou's back yard. Their small frame house was on the edge of the sleepy farm town which bordered the swamp.

Jessica was just a summer visitor. Her real home

was in a crowded city up north. Jessica's father had died in a factory accident when she was a baby and she and her hard-working mother lived on a street her mother always said had gone from bad to worse. Every summer she tried to get Jessica away to the country.

'It will be hot down there, Jessica,' she'd said as she packed Jessica's little suitcase. 'But your cousin Andrew has a shady back yard and cousin Mary Lou keeps rabbits and chickens and ducks. Be helpful and be sure to be nice to your little cousin Hokey.'

Hokey turned out to be four years old and a brat but otherwise the summer had been fun. Cousin Andrew had twice taken everyone to the beach fifty miles away and Jessica had seen the sea for the first time ever.

Now it was all over. In a little while, she would have to take off her blue jeans and T-shirt and put on her travelling dress and shoes, wash her face and brush her hair. Then cousin Andrew would walk her to the bus station carrying her suitcase.

Jessica missed her mother quite badly and it should have been a happy day but instead it was the most awful day she could ever remember.

That was because of Gribit. She scooped him up from by her feet and, cuddling him close, sat down on a moss-covered fallen tree.

Gribit was a baby duck only six weeks old. The day Jessica arrived, cousin Andrew's old mallard hatched a dozen fluffy balls of yellow. Jessica rescued a thirteenth just as cousin Hokey tried to smash it with his red beach shovel. The duckling wasn't able to break out of its shell, and, peering through a hole pecked from the inside Jessica had seen a tiny yellow beak gasping for air. Very carefully, she released the little prisoner and took it to her room to give it water and keep it warm.

It turned out to be a little drake. She called him

Gribit because of the little reedy 'Gribit-grabit' sound he made whenever he wanted something, and soon he was following every step she took. He would have nothing to do with the other ducks and at night slept on her pillow nestled against her head.

'You've become his mother, Jessica,' cousin Mary Lou said. 'He thinks he's a human being like you.'

'Silly old Gribit,' Jessica whispered tearfully. 'What are we going to do? You're nowhere near ready to be on your own yet.' She stroked the tiny pin-feathers that would some day turn into the lovely shiny waterproof cape worn by big ducks.

Without her, she knew, he would not eat and only yesterday she had caught cousin Hokey holding him under water in the paddling pool to see how long he could go without breathing. A grown up world, however, had decided a tiny city apartment was no place for a duck. Jessica had never felt so helpless. The harder she tried to think of some way to save her 'child', the less she was able to.

Unconcerned, Gribit happily snapped his little beak shut on a passing mosquito.

A gravelly voice suddenly shattered the swamp's silence. 'What did you call him? Grubber? Grabber? Gribbit? What a peculiar name.'

Jessica's heart nearly stopped. Who on earth was that? She looked around cautiously. A dragonfly hissed by. Not far away a heron flapped his white wings to dry them. The voice had come from misty shadows near the end of the moss-covered tree trunk she was seated on.

'Who – who's there?' she demanded timorously.

'I am,' the voice answered unhelpfully. 'And what are you so unhappy about? You're crying a lot, you know.'

Jessica wiped away tears to see better. Sure enough, there *was* someone there. It was someone wearing wellington boots, faded blue jeans and a slightly tattered yellow waistcoat with big brass buttons.

'I'm *not* crying,' she said firmly. 'And who are you, anyway?'

The figure made a low bow. 'Alfred. That's my name. And at your service. You are not by any chance a princess, are you?'

'Of course not,' Jessica said, quite surprised by the question.

'Oh,' said the stranger. He sounded disappointed.

Jessica peered more closely. She saw a face that seemed almost all nose, teeth which looked suspiciously pointed, eyes close to the top of a flattened head and bumpy skin that was brown-green.

Oddest of all, she thought she saw a tail. A rather heavy scaly one. But that was impossible, she told herself – although her mother always said nothing was impossible and that life was filled with extraordinary surprises.

'I beg your pardon,' she said, trying not to sound too frightened although she was ready to run if the strange figure came one step closer. 'You are not by any chance an alligator, are you?'

The gravelly voice at once became indignant. 'An alligator? Me? I should hope not!'

'Oh,' said Jessica hurriedly. 'I'm sorry.' She felt a little foolish as well as relieved. Of course he couldn't be an alligator. What alligator talked and was named Alfred? Or for that matter wore wellington boots and a yellow waistcoat and blue jeans?

'You're forgiven,' came the pleasant reply. 'Although I should have thought it perfectly clear what I am.'

Something in his manner annoyed Jessica. She didn't think it at all clear and when she suddenly saw a long scaly tail again, she told him so.

'Nonsense!' he declared. 'You don't know the first thing about natural history.'

'I do, too,' Jessica argued.

'You don't,' he repeated. 'Because if you did . . .' he drew himself up to his full height and puffed out his chest . . . 'you would have known at once that I am that proudest of all nature's wonders, a crocodile.'

2

'Acrocodile!' exclaimed Jessica. 'But that's impossible. Crocodiles come from Africa.'

Then she remembered and backed away. Crocodile *or* alligator, this could be the way little girls were lured to the water's edge.

'You're quite right,' agreed the other cheerfully. 'And Africa is where I was going. I'd heard there was a princess in trouble there, you see. But I seem to have jumped into the wrong whirlpool.' He scratched his bumpy green forehead with a webby finger. 'There were two of them,' he went on, 'and "eeny-meeny-miny-moe" didn't come out right.'

'Whirlpool?' Jessica asked. She felt completely confused. It had just occurred to her she was finding it quite normal that a crocodile could talk.

'The one on the "other side",' she heard him explain.

'The "other side" of what?' she demanded.

'The "other side" of here, of course,' was the reply and the crocodile pointed straight down. 'Everything has at least two sides, doesn't it?' he asked. 'This is one side, up here. I come from the "other side", down there.'

'The "other side" of here,' Jessica shot back, 'after

you go through the boiling-hot middle of the earth, is China. That's almost the first thing you learn in school.'

'School!' snorted the crocodile. 'Once they taught everyone the world was flat.'

Jessica decided there was no point in arguing. She glanced down the path again. Cousin Andrew had appeared in the back yard, looking around. That meant it was nearly time for her bus. In a few minutes she would have to leave Gribit forever.

She began to cry once more.

'Dear, dear, there you go again,' said the crocodile. 'What on earth is the matter? Is it an ogre? Or perhaps a giant?'

'Don't be silly!' Jessica sobbed. 'There aren't any such things.'

'Or is it a witch?' he asked, going right on. 'Last week I had the most awful trouble with a horrible one who lived in a cave and wore red. When I chopped off her head her body ran into the woods, leaving her head all by itself screaming for help. Can you im- agine?'

Jessica could not. She shook her head and said brokenly, 'Please, I don't want to talk to anyone. Won't you go away?'

Instead, the crocodile came and sat alarmingly close, his webby thumbs hooked into the pockets of his yellow waistcoat. 'Perhaps,' he said in a kindly tone, 'if you told me what the matter was I could help. It's to do with Gribit, isn't it? Did you rescue him from an egg?'

'Yes,' sniffed Jessica, surprised. 'How did you know?' And then, before she knew it, she was telling him all about how she had raised Gribit and was going home in a few minutes and had to leave him behind.

11

He listened carefully, only saying 'Ah . . .' from time to time, and 'Hmmmm . . .'

When she had finished, he sat a moment, clearly deep in thought. Suddenly he leapt to his feet. 'Got it!' he cried joyfully. 'In another month Gribit will be grown up enough to take care of himself, won't he? And be safe from cousin Hokey.'

Jessica nodded numbly. 'I – I guess so . . .'

'Then,' he exclaimed grandly, 'all you have to do is stay with me for a month on the "other side".'

It was so unexpected, Jessica simply stared.

'Of course, you would miss some school,' the crocodile went on in his gravelly voice. 'But what's school compared to Gribit?' With one green webby finger he chucked the little duckling under his beak.

'Gribit-gribit-gribit,' peeped Gribit. Quite unafraid, he snapped at another passing mosquito.

Jessica finally began to think clearly. You didn't ever go anywhere with strangers, no matter how friendly they were. As for going off somewhere with a crocodile, even one who could talk, that was out of the question.

'All you have to do,' he was saying, 'is jump in, right here.' He pointed at a dark, silent pool nearby. 'That's where I came up. See? The whirlpool is just starting again.'

Sure enough, the water had begun to turn slowly in wide circles.

'Jessica!' Cousin Andrew's voice came down the narrow path. 'Where are you? We'll be late.'

Cousin Mary Lou had joined him. They studied the path where it entered the swamp.

'Hurry!' said the crocodile. 'They've discovered Gribit's tracks.'

He strode quickly to the pool and Jessica noticed for

12

the first time, heaped on the ground, what appeared to be a pile of battered armour, the kind knights wore in the old days.

'This goes first,' the crocodile said. He grabbed up a badly-dented shield emblazoned with a big green crocodile head.

'It's only brass,' he apologized. 'But some day, when I am officially knighted, I'll have armour of real gold.'

He threw the shield in the water which was now whirling around faster and faster. It disappeared at once.

'Oh, oh, here they come!' He pointed. Indeed, cousin Andrew was half-way down the path with cousin Mary Lou right behind him. 'If they see me,' he said, 'you won't stand a chance.'

A breastplate followed the shield, then a visored helmet bedecked with a long green feather, then brass shin guards.

Now the whirling water made a deep moaning sound. The crocodile brandished a long double-bladed sword. 'Ready?' he cried. 'You first. I'll hold off the enemy.'

'Jessica! What on earth are you doing out there?' Cousin Andrew had finally spotted her.

'Hurry!' growled the crocodile. 'It's now or never.'

But Jessica didn't move. She couldn't. Her mind had stopped. It was all too much.

'All right,' was the cry. 'We'll go first, then.' One big webby hand snatched Gribit from her arms. And with that, the crocodile dived directly into the water.

Jessica came to life. What dreadful thing was happening to her child? 'Gribit!' she screamed. Without a second thought, she dived head first after him and the dark water closed immediately over her.

13

'Jessica?' Cousin Andrew and cousin Mary Lou looked horrified at the whirling water. Jessica's footprints and the prints of a large pair of rubber boots went right to the edge of the bank above the whirlpool.

A heron flapped. Mosquitoes droned. But of Jessica and Gribit there was not a single trace, except for one little downy duckling feather that floated forlornly around and around until the dark waters finally stilled.

3

I t was all very confusing.

One moment, Jessica was holding her breath in pitch darkness. There was a terrible roar of water and she was knocked to and fro as though being punched by big wet pillows.

The next moment, she found herself standing up in a clear, bubbling brook which ran through a warm sunlit meadow of pretty wild flowers. A path from a dark wood beyond came over a rickety bridge to a white picket fence surrounding an old stone cottage where cosy windows peeped out from under a roof of thatched straw.

Good heavens, thought Jessica, this must be the 'other side'. She looked around expectantly, but of Gribit there was not a sign. Nor of the crocodile who called himself Alfred, wore jeans, a brass-buttoned yellow waistcoat and wellington boots, and carried around battered brass armour.

Jessica called anxiously. 'Gribit . . .?'

There was no familiar peeping answer. She scrambled out of the brook and called again.

This time, a reply suddenly came from a nearby oak

tree. 'Gribit, gribit, gribit,' a voice shouted. And there was some rather rude laughter.

Jessica looked up and saw three crows standing on a branch. They wore shabby overalls and old hats full of holes and their feathers looked moth-eaten.

'Please!' asked Jessica. 'Did you see a little duckling?' She found she wasn't in the least surprised that the crows were dressed.

One who seemed to be the leader shouted again:

> 'Ducky-Wucky, not so lucky,
> Ducky-Wucky went quack-quack,
> Ducky swam down through a whirlpool,
> Ducky-Wucky never came back.'

At this, his friends nearly fell off the branch laughing. They reminded Jessica of men she'd seen back home stumbling out of a bar down the street very late at night. In fact, didn't one have a rather suspicious bottle of something tucked under his wing?

'I. . .I think you're horrid,' she cried.

Ignoring their hoots and whistles, she ran along the edge of the brook, looking again for Gribit. Just by the cottage where freshly-washed laundry was hanging out on a clothes line to dry, she called once more.

'Gribit . . .!!!'

'He was here just a moment ago,' a kindly voice said, matter-of-factly. 'Sitting on Alfred's head when he came up out of the whirlpool.'

Jessica peered around. The voice had come from behind what she first thought were pillowcases but which turned out to be an enormous pair of old-fashioned ladies bloomers with pink, lacy frills at the bottom of each leg.

Their owner suddenly appeared from behind them

and Jessica found herself staring at someone very big and fat who wore a freshly-starched apron over a clean white summer dress embroidered with little blue cornflowers. She smelled of laundry soap and ironing. She had large hoof-like hands, her skin was a rich dark brown like old saddle-leather and her wide smile showed a large pink tongue and some rather prominent front teeth.

In fact, she looked for all the world like a hippopotamus.

Jessica didn't have time to think about that, however. Her new acquaintance called out, 'Alfred! The little duck's mother is here!'

The crocodile's now familiar gravelly voice came back at once from among some reeds by the brook. 'I've lost my helmet,' it shouted.

Almost immediately, however, Jessica heard the sort of pleased exclamation which said something lost and important was finally found and Alfred reared up out of the reeds waving the brass helmet with its green plume now very bedraggled.

'Found it,' he cried.

'Where's Gribit?' demanded Jessica crossly.

'He's under the bridge,' replied Alfred, 'chasing a fish.'

He came from the brook carrying all his armour, water streaming from his clothes and squishing up out of his wellingtons.

Jessica waded frantically into the quiet water beneath the bridge – and to her overwhelming relief, there was Gribit, ruffling his new pin-feathers and stabbing at a darting water spider. Coming down through a whirlpool didn't seem to have bothered him at all.

'Enough swimming for you today,' Jessica ordered.

She scooped him up and carried him out. 'That was a dirty trick,' she said to the crocodile, 'snatching him from me like that.'

'If I hadn't,' he declared, 'you would be on the bus right now, heading north alone.'

Jessica had no answer. It was the truth. Without a doubt he had saved Gribit's life.

The big hippopotamus lady sighed and said, 'Alfred's always rescuing someone. Some day it will be a real princess and he finally will be knighted.'

'Why does it have to be a princess?' asked Jessica.

'Because,' was the reply, 'that is the rule on this side. And a rule is a rule.'

The hippopotamus picked up a laundry basket full of freshly-dried clothes. 'You're soaking wet and swampy,' she observed in a motherly way. 'Perhaps you would like a hot bath while I wash and dry your things.'

Jessica, who now felt shivery cold, thought that was a good idea. With Gribit nestled in her arms, she followed the hippopotamus. For the first time she was aware of great silence. Except for the brook there was not a sound.

'Don't you have cars on this side?' she inquired.

'No, child. Nor trains, nor aeroplanes.'

'Why not?' Jessica demanded.

'They're dangerous,' was the answer.

Jessica didn't think she could argue with that. They went up a brick walk bordered with pretty flowers. Hanging over the front door was a wooden sign which said in old letters 'Hannah's Haven'.

'Are you Hannah?' she guessed.

The hippopotamus lady nodded. 'I take in boarders and sometimes a traveller who looks for a good supper. I'm a widow, you see.'

18

'My name is Jessica,' said Jessica politely. 'Does the crocodile – does Alfred live here, too?'

'When he's not off rescuing someone,' was the reply. 'But of course, most of the time he is. There are so many giants and witches and ogres misbehaving themselves these days.'

'Real ones?' Jessica asked. She started also to ask if an ogre or a giant wasn't just as dangerous as a car or aeroplane, but a shout interrupted her.

> 'Join an ogre for dinner,
> Share a stew!
> Just be careful,
> The stew isn't you!'

It was the crow again. He and his two tattered friends had flown down to perch on the sign over the door.

'Shoo!' cried Hannah. She waved a broom. 'Naughty creatures. You'll end up in a pot yourselves.'

The crows flapped away, hooting and cackling.

'Alfred rescued them,' Hannah explained, 'from a pie in a sorcerer's kitchen. If I could ever catch them I'd make him take them back.' She went inside.

Jessica hesitated, holding Gribit tightly. It was all so strange: witches, giants, ogres, sorcerers. Because she had never seen any, it didn't mean they did not exist. After all, she'd already met a crocodile who wanted to be a knight, a hippopotamus who took in boarders and crows who drank from a suspicious bottle and shouted horrid rhymes.

She looked around, half-expecting to see something dreadful appear from the dark wood beyond the meadow. But all she saw was Alfred hanging up his armour on Hannah's washing line and whistling a cheerful tune. So she hurried after the hippopotamus.

4

J essica found herself in a charming low-ceilinged
room where there was a crackling wood fire and
an old oak table flanked by benches. Pots and
pans and bunches of herbs hung from rough-
hewn beams. A casement window looked on to a
vegetable garden. Under it was a washtub and nearby
an old-fashioned iron stove on which a simmering pot
gave off a delicious odour of soup.

Hannah put down her laundry, took up an enormous steaming kettle and started up a winding stair.
Jessica followed.

At the end of a short hall, they entered a little guest
room whose slanted ceiling and curtained window told
Jessica she was directly under the thatched roof.
There was a comfortable-looking bed covered with a
soft patchwork quilt, a wooden washstand with a
porcelain bowl and jug, a pine chest and a tin bath-
tub just big enough to sit in.

'Here we are,' said Hannah. She poured the kettle
into the bath and politely turned her back as Jessica
took off her wet things.

'Why does Alfred want to be a knight?' Jessica
asked.

'Why not?' was the answer. 'Everyone always dreams of being *something*, don't they? A great general, say, or a sea captain or an explorer?'

'But he acts like a knight already,' protested Jessica, 'always rescuing somebody or fighting someone wicked.'

'The professor says,' replied the hippopotamus, 'it's one thing to *be* something and quite another to have a title that tells everyone you *are*. A title makes being something *official* and that's very important, you know.' She sighed. 'Poor Alfred, he's been disappointed so often. He'd even heard I was a princess.'

'Oh,' said Jessica. 'Did he rescue you, too?'

'Yes, dear. From a terrible place called a zoo. And the professor, too. He saved him from cannibals who were just about to cook him for lunch.'

'Who is the professor?' asked Jessica.

'My other boarder,' replied Hannah mysteriously. She gathered Jessica's wet clothes. 'Dinner will be at six,' she said and left, closing the door behind her.

Jessica got in the bath and Gribit came and perched on her knees.

'Everyone else talks,' she said to him. 'Why can't you? You're old enough now.'

'Gribit, gribit,' he said.

Jessica shook her head. She would ask Hannah.

After a while she felt terribly sleepy. She dried off with a big towel and lay down on the bed, pulling the patchwork quilt up over her. Soft sunlight came through the window, a fly buzzed, she could hear the hippopotamus singing downstairs in the kitchen and the thump-thump of clothes being hand-washed. Gribit nestled close to her the way he always did.

She began to think of her mother. She must be certain something dreadful had happened to her

21

daughter, disappearing all of a sudden in the swamp; and she wished there were some way she could let her know everything was all right. Home seemed a million miles away and she guessed the only way to get back there was to dive into the whirlpool again.

But suppose by the time Gribit was old enough to care for himself it had stopped whirling? Or suppose she ended up in Africa by mistake, the way the crocodile had ended up in America?

Jessica's thoughts went around and around, and then she fell asleep.

When she woke she thought she was dreaming, for the face that stared at her from close by had a huge beak protruding from under large steel-rimmed spectacles behind which piercing eyes left her face only to glance down at a large and dusty dictionary.

Then she saw her clothes, freshly washed and folded neatly on a chair, and knew she wasn't dreaming and that the beak belonged to some sort of a bird as big as an ostrich.

'Ha!' it said abruptly in highly-educated tones. 'I thought so. You are an immature homo sapiens of the female gender.'

There was a bang as the dictionary was shut.

Jessica sat up.

The feathered creature wore a starched high collar and the sort of suit worn many years ago by doctors, lawyers and men of great learning; striped grey and black trousers, a pearl-grey waistcoat and a black jacket with long tails which had to be flipped up out of the way when the wearer sat down.

'Why,' exclaimed Jessica, astonished, 'you're a dodo bird.'

The creature nodded stiffly. 'At your service, P.B.'

'What does P.B. stand for?' asked Jessica.

'Professor of Books, of course,' was the reply.

'But dodo birds don't exist any longer,' Jessica protested. 'You're extinct.'

'Perhaps where you come from.' The dodo bird clacked his beak snappishly. 'But on *this* side we obviously are not, for here I am.' He tucked the dictionary under one wing, gathered up several encyclopaedias and went to the door. 'Supper is ready,' he announced.

'What's an immature homo sapiens of the female gender?' Jessica called after him.

'A little girl human being,' he called back and the door closed behind him.

Jessica giggled and jumped from the bed. In spite of his brusque manner, the Professor of Books appeared quite harmless.

She went to the window and looked out. The sun had set, twilight was turning to night. She quickly splashed water on her face and went down the winding stair.

The hippopotamus was removing some freshly baked bread from the oven. It smelled delicious. She had tied a pink ribbon around a few wispy hairs that grew from the top of her head and had put on a fresh apron.

'Sit opposite the professor,' she told Jessica. 'And your child next to you. He must be hungry, poor little boy.'

'Thank you,' said Jessica, and remembered the question she wanted to ask. 'Hannah, why can't Gribit talk?'

'Because, dear, he belongs to *your* side,' Hannah explained. 'Only animals who belong to *this* side can talk.'

'Oh,' said Jessica a little sadly. 'Poor Gribit.'

23

Gribit snapped at a house fly. His place was a tall stack of cushions which reached right up to the table. He at once dug his little bill into a plate of assorted seeds.

'Alfred,' cried Hannah as she brought the bread.

'At present he is resting in the arms of Morpheus resuscitating energy expended by his labours,' remarked the dodo bird wisely.

'I suppose that means he's tired and sleeping,' Jessica said. 'He certainly looks it.'

The crocodile was indeed asleep, slumped at a place near the fire, his long chin resting on the table.

'Precisely,' agreed the dodo. He opened up his heavy dictionary. 'Wake up, sir!' he commanded and slammed the book shut.

Alfred leapt to his feet as though shot. 'Fill in the moat!' he cried. 'Storm the walls! Batter down the portcullis!'

'Soup is ready,' Hannah said patiently. She put a big steaming bowl of it on the table.

'Oh,' said Alfred. He sat back down. 'I was dreaming,' he said.

'You were assaulting a castle, I believe,' remarked the dodo, clacking his beak.

'A princess was a prisoner in the donjon,' said Alfred. He took up a spoon and slurped some soup, a little noisily, Jessica thought.

'A donjon,' explained the feathered Professor of Books, 'is the centre tower of a fortress castle. It should not be confused with a similar word, "dungeon", which describes a small windowless underground prison. One is *up*, you see, the other *down*, and . . .'

A knock on the front door interrupted him. They all turned. Hannah said pleasantly, 'Come in . . .'

24

The door creaked open. An old woman entered, blinking at the sudden light. She wore long skirts and a threadbare sweater worn through at the elbows. A tattered shawl was tied around her head. In one hand she carried a shabby suitcase and in the other a furled umbrella which was torn in several places.

Gribit, with a shrill peep of fear, leapt off his cushions and into Jessica's arms.

'Gribit,' she whispered. 'Behave . . .' But she didn't say it very firmly for she felt an unexplained chill herself at the old woman's presence, as though a cold dark wind had blown through the door behind her bringing a sense of mould and damp and something else Jessica could only think of as evil.

5

The old woman was, in fact, a rat and nearly as big as Jessica. Her eyes were small and red. Two wide yellow front teeth stuck out over her lower lip and a thin hairless tail came from below her skirts and wrapped around feet whose toenails were very long and curved.

'I'm travelling from one end of this side to the other,' she announced in a quavering voice. 'And I've had nothing to eat since yesterday morning.'

'There's only vegetable soup, I'm afraid,' said Hannah. 'And home-made bread.'

But the old rat woman had already put down her suitcase and umbrella and hung her tattered shawl on a peg by the door. Without a word, she hobbled to an empty place and Hannah served her although a little reluctantly, Jessica thought.

Alfred cleared his throat and asked politely, 'Do you come from the *very* End?'

'Yes,' was the answer. 'From the very, *very* End.'

'I've never been that far,' declared Alfred wistfully.

'The *very* End is across the Pirate Sea, I believe,' intoned the dodo. 'And then across the Empty Desert where I've read there is a cyclops.'

'What's a cyclops?' asked Jessica.

'A one-eyed ogre,' said Alfred. 'The eye is in the centre of its forehead.' He turned to the Professor of Books. 'Why can't you ever speak plain English?' he complained.

'Because,' was the immediate answer, 'we don't live in Plain England.'

Jessica saw an argument coming and hurriedly found courage to question the old woman herself. 'What's at the *very* End?' she asked.

'The Bottomless Lake, child, whose water is as black as night. The very, *very* End is in the middle of it.'

'Then it must be an island,' exclaimed Jessica. 'Who lives there?'

But at that the old rat woman looked strangely frightened. 'It could be dangerous for you to know,' she murmured and her little red eyes glanced sideways.

'Fiddle!' cried Alfred, snapping his fingers to show he was afraid of nothing.

'Danger,' declared the dodo with a clack of his big beak, 'is relative. That means what might be dangerous to *you* might *not* be dangerous to my friend here.'

Jessica clean forgot herself. 'Why,' she burst out proudly, 'just the other day, Alfred cut off the head of a mean old witch and the body went running into the woods all by itself.' Then she remembered she was at dinner. 'Oh!' she apologized. 'Excuse me.'

But Alfred rose to make a gallant bow. 'Thank you,' he beamed.

The old rat woman appeared to change her mind. 'Very well,' she said, 'but you must promise you will never reveal you learned it from me.'

'On my honour,' cried Alfred.

Jessica and the dodo nodded. Only Hannah at the stove gave no sign and that was because she couldn't hear.

The old rat woman looked carefully around and lowered her voice. 'Lady Gleam lives there,' she said. Then she bent quickly over her soup again and her hand shook so hard her spoon rattled against her bowl.

Jessica glanced at the crocodile but Alfred clearly had no idea who Lady Gleam was. Nor, apparently, had the dodo. The worthy professor had opened one of his dusty volumes to try to find out.

'Who *is* Lady Gleam?' asked Jessica. 'Why are you so frightened of her?'

The little red eyes darted. 'Because, my dear,' the old rat answered, 'I know of her prisoner.'

Alfred was instantly all ears. 'Prisoner? What prisoner?'

'Shhhh . . .!' warned the old rat. 'Who knows what Lady Gleam can hear?' She leaned forward and they all strained to catch every word. 'The princess, of course,' she whispered.

Alfred leapt to his feet. 'A princess?' he cried. 'A real one?'

'Such a pretty thing, too,' the old rat said. 'To get her back, her poor father must pay a ransom in gold equal to her weight. But every time he comes to pay it, Lady Gleam has fattened the princess up and he finds he hasn't brought enough.'

'But that's awful,' cried Jessica. She clutched Gribit close.

'Ha!' exclaimed the dodo, touching a dusty page with one claw. 'Lady Gleam, sorceress, black magic, etcetera . . . Hmmmm . . . She is said to take many forms, from serpent to human, and sometimes to be

28

only a cold black wind, etcetera . . . Hmmmm . . .' He frowned suddenly. 'Oh dear,' he said. 'She only eats but once a year, and then it's to feast off the heart of a fresh-killed child of royal blood.'

'The princess!' exclaimed Jessica.

She turned horrified eyes to Alfred but before he could speak they heard Hannah say pleasantly, 'That will be one coin, please.' And there was the chink of money. It was the old rat woman paying for her soup.

'Wait!' commanded Alfred.

'I've said enough,' muttered the rat. She hid her purse under her long skirts, hurriedly drew on her shawl and seized up her suitcase and umbrella. But as she threw open the door to rush out, Gribit, excited by her flight, leapt from Jessica's arms and chased after her flying feet.

'Gribit,' cried Jessica.

Too late. Avoiding him, the old woman tripped. With a shriek, she sprawled headlong on the brick walk.

'Cursed bird!' she screamed. She scrambled up, aimed a wild kick at Gribit and ran to her suitcase which had burst open. Jessica, who'd come to the rescue, could hardly believe what she saw lying in it. On top of some dirty clothes was a long fat string of sausages and a loaf of bread. Next to them was something even more extraordinary, a large and very dangerous-looking pistol.

'Mind your own business, child!' snarled the rat. She gnashed her yellow teeth, slammed the suitcase shut and rushed off into the night.

Jessica picked up Gribit and went back indoors, her mind spinning. The old woman could not have been hungry at all. And why was she carrying a deadly pistol?

Hannah locked the door behind her. The crocodile had joined the dodo at his dusty book. Both were reading furiously.

'I think we had better leave the gentlemen to their studying,' Hannah said. She lit a candle and turned to go upstairs. 'We'll be leaving first thing in the morning.'

'Where are we going?' asked Jessica, even though she guessed what the answer would be.

'Why, to Lady Gleam's,' answered the hippopotamus matter-of-factly. 'To rescue the princess.'

6

Hannah woke Jessica and Gribit at first light. Last night she had explained why Jessica had to join the expedition to Lady Gleam's. 'It might not be safe for you here if the old rat returned and found you alone,' she said.

'Do you always go with Alfred on "rescues"?' Jessica now asked as she dressed quickly. She could not imagine the big hippopotamus crossing deserts and mountains.

'Most times,' replied Hannah. 'If I didn't, who would see he changed his socks every day?' As for the professor, she went on to explain, he usually went, too. It was to gather fresh knowledge to put in his books so they wouldn't be quite so dusty. Jessica suspected, however, that the real reason for both of them was the excitement.

Downstairs she found Alfred and the dodo already at breakfast.

'It may be our last one for some time,' declared Alfred cheerfully. And he threw four slices of toast into his mouth at once. He'd been up for an hour, polishing his armour and sharpening his sword. When Jessica told him about the sausages and bread and pistol she'd seen in the old rat's suitcase, it didn't make him or the dodo the least bit suspicious.

'She was probably saving the food for an emergency,' the crocodile said.

'Carrying a pistol makes good sense when there are pirates about,' remarked the dodo wisely.

But Jessica couldn't help thinking that for some reason they were being tricked.

Breakfast over, Alfred tied up his armour in a neat bundle to be carried over his shoulder. The dodo carefully arranged a few important volumes in a knapsack. Hannah packed a carpet bag with tooth-brushes and washing powder and a change of clothes for everyone. Then she put on her best sun bonnet and a fresh apron and locked the front door.

As the sun rose, they set off for the dark woods beyond the meadow. Crossing the brook, Jessica hesitated. It was her last chance to dive back through the whirlpool and go home to her mother. Then Gribit wriggled in her arms, hoping to swim again.

'Oh, Gribit, you silly duck,' Jessica said lovingly and she hurried after the others.

Alfred led the way, whistling cheerfully. The dodo came second with a compass and, since there was no path to follow, from time to time he would give directions. 'East-north-east,' he would order, learn-edly. Or, 'East a quarter point south.'

'Don't you have roads on this side?' Jessica asked.

'Of course not,' snapped the Professor of Books. 'Roads only lead from one place to another perhaps no better.'

At noon, they stopped by a pretty waterfall and Hannah produced sandwiches from her carpet bag.

'How will we cross the Pirate Sea?' Jessica asked Alfred.

'We shall build a raft,' he declared.

'Perhaps,' said Jessica, 'Gribit and I will bring you luck and you will be knighted finally.'

In the afternoon, the woods grew darker and the way harder. Nobody talked. It seemed to Jessica they would never get there. Once a raucous scream made them all look up.

The three crows were seated on a branch above and drinking from their suspicious bottle.

> 'Roses are red,
> Violets are pink!
> The ocean's farther away
> Than you think.'

'You promised to leave them behind,' Hannah said accusingly to Alfred.

'Go home,' he shouted. He threw up a pine cone and they flapped away. 'Don't listen to them,' he said. 'We'll be there by sundown.'

Sure enough, just as the sun was setting, they heard the far-off whispery sound of waves pounding the shore. They hurried on and soon came to a beach of pure white sand. Beyond it lay a vast and empty expanse of blue water.

'The Pirate Sea!' shouted Alfred triumphantly.

While Jessica and Hannah gathered wood for a fire, he got to work to make a shelter. The dodo, meanwhile, produced a length of twine and some hooks and with the help of some horrid crawling things he found under a rock, began to fish.

In no time, a warm fire crackled in front of a cosy lean-to. Fish sizzled on the big flat rock Hannah used as a frying pan and a delicious smell came from some steamy seaweed in which she had wrapped clams and mussels.

After they had eaten, the stars came out, hanging big and bright in an inky black sky. Alfred and the dodo studied the map. Jessica cuddled against Hannah and Gribit, who had eaten a whole plateful of worms, fell contentedly asleep on her lap. The last thing Jessica remembered was the freshly laundered smell of Hannah's dress and apron.

When she awoke it was dawn. The crocodile was asleep by the burned-out fire, his head pillowed on dry seaweed. The dodo, feathers spilling out from his frock coat, had his head twisted about in his high collar and tucked under his wing. Up in a tree were three silent ragged shapes that Jessica guessed were the crows. Next to her, Hannah breathed slowly and deeply.

Suddenly Jessica missed Gribit. Where was he? She rose quietly and soon saw the tracks of his little webbed feet going up the beach. She followed them anxiously. After a while she turned a point of land which cut her friends from view. And there indeed was Gribit, pecking away at sand shrimps. But beyond him there was something else, something that made Jessica's heart nearly stop.

Anchored just off shore was a big sailing ship. Flying from the tallest of its three masts was a black flag with a white skull-and-crossbones on it. Closer, clustered around the ship's long boat drawn up on the beach, were a dozen wicked-looking pirates. One had a beard and wore gold earrings, another had an iron hook in place of a hand. All carried terrible cutlasses and huge pistols.

Jessica could hardly find her voice. 'Gribit,' she whispered. She ran silently up to him. 'Gribit. Quick!'

She had just bent to pick him up when she heard

someone behind her. Before she could turn, a huge dirty hand was clamped over her mouth and she was lifted high off the sand.

'Ha, mates!' a cruel voice roared. 'Look what we have here!'

Jessica kicked and struggled but it was too late. She was tumbled head-over-heels into a foul-smelling sack. She heard roars of glee. Big fingers poked at her, and then she flew through the air and landed on her head against something very hard.

After that she knew nothing.

7

When Jessica came to her senses she had a terrible headache. Someone was holding a cold cloth to her forehead and a gentle voice was saying, 'You'll feel better soon. You were thrown into the pirates' long boat and knocked out.'

Jessica opened her eyes and saw by the weak light of an oil-lamp hanging from the low ceiling that she was in a narrow bunk in a small prison-like room. There was a smell of tar and rope. The lamp swayed and there was a sound of moving water and a distant moan of wind. All told Jessica she was in the pirate ship.

She turned her head and saw seated on the edge of the bunk the most beautiful girl she could ever have imagined. Her eyes were a deep sea-green colour. Long dark hair framed a face as delicate as a young deer's and spilled down in waves to cover bare shoulders. A slender body whose skin was the colour and smoothness of pearls ended just below the waist in a long fish's tail, its scales gleaming like the finest silver.

'Why, you're a mermaid,' said Jessica.

'Yes,' the other replied simply. 'And I am their prisoner, too.'

'What's your name?'

'I don't have one,' replied the mermaid. 'Sea people never do. We speak with our minds instead of our mouths so we don't need names.'

'I'm Jessica,' said Jessica, and added hopefully, 'Have you seen Gribit? He's my little duck.'

The mermaid shook her head. 'Nobody came from the beach with the pirates except you,' she declared.

Jessica brightened. 'That probably means he escaped back to Alfred. Alfred's a crocodile.' Then she added quickly, 'But not an ordinary one.'

The mermaid nodded. 'The pirates said they were old enemies. They left a message for him on the beach. He can either take your place here or he can pay a ransom for you. He has just one week to make up his mind. If he can't . . .' The mermaid's sea-green eyes suddenly misted with frightened tears.

Jessica said bravely, 'We won't think of "if he can't", because Alfred *will* rescue us, you'll see.'

'Of course he will.' The mermaid quickly wiped her tears away with a strand of her beautiful hair. 'And if for some reason he doesn't, we'll escape, although I haven't had much success so far.'

She told Jessica how she was captured: 'I climbed up on a rock to comb my hair,' she said, 'and the next thing I knew I was in a net.' She laughed and it was like the tinkling of a wind-chime made of delicate sea shells. 'And now,' she went on, 'how about you? Aren't you from the "other side"?'

Her smile was so sweet that Jessica at once told her the whole story, from her mother sending her to her cousin for the summer to the old rat woman and her strange tale of Lady Gleam and a princess prisoner. 'I think it's some sort of trick,' she exclaimed. 'Though I can't understand it.'

'Don't try to now,' said the mermaid. She put a cool hand on Jessica's head. 'You must rest,' she ordered.

Jessica obeyed and closed her eyes. But she didn't sleep. How could her friends ever raise the kind of ransom the pirates must have demanded? And why should Alfred ever sacrifice his life for her? Because if he did change places with her the pirates would certainly dispose of him in the most awful manner. She would have to think of some way to escape.

A shattering noise interrupted her thoughts. The door to the cabin burst open. It was the pirate captain himself. He had a wooden leg and a thick red beard which was plastered with rotting food. He had gold earrings and black pointed teeth and wore a black bandanna tied tightly around his hair. His clothes were thick with grease and dirt and an ugly pistol was shoved into his broad belt.

'Avast ye, there,' he growled. 'There's work to be done.'

Before either Jessica or the mermaid could resist, he locked them together with heavy iron handcuffs. 'Now, up on deck you go,' he bellowed. And he seized the mermaid by the hair and dragged her out into a narrow passageway and up a steep ladder.

Jessica was pulled along behind and they burst out into bright sunshine, to be roughly thrown down on the deck before two buckets filled with cold salt water. Around them, the sea was empty of sail or sign of land.

'Scrub!' the captain shouted. He threw down two heavy brushes.

Without a murmur, the mermaid took up one and began to wash the deck. Jessica followed her lead. The moment the pirate turned his back, however, she whispered, 'This was his first mistake. The more he takes us out of that cabin, the more he'll get used to us and watch us less carefully. Then we'll have a better chance.'

As each day passed, however, no chance appeared. Every dawn, Jessica and the mermaid were handcuffed together and made to slave until dusk, when their only reward was stale bread and some watery foul-tasting soup. Soon, both grew quite ill.

All the time the pirates stood about gleefully counting off the days remaining and making cruel remarks about their fate. Jessica and the mermaid bravely tried to keep each other's courage up. At night, however, Jessica found it hard not to cry herself to sleep. She missed her mother dreadfully. Then she would think of little Gribit. Had he really been able to escape back to her friends? And what had happened to them? It didn't seem possible she would never see them again.

Time finally ran out, their last day came to an end. 'Tonight,' the pirate captain roared, 'is your last!'

He dragged them below for the final time to their little prison. 'Sleep well,' he laughed. He removed their handcuffs, slammed the door behind him and headed back up on deck.

As his footsteps faded, the mermaid and Jessica turned excited faces to each other, hardly believing their luck. Just as Jessica had predicted, the pirate had become so used to them he'd grown careless. The chance they had been waiting for had finally come.

He had forgotten to lock their door.

8

'We must wait until after midnight,' said the mermaid. 'Then everyone will be in their bunks except the helmsman, and he will be sleepy.'

They had decided to steal the pirates' long boat. 'I don't know what will happen to us out there,' said Jessica, 'but I'd rather drown or die of thirst than face whatever the pirates have in store for us.'

The time ticked slowly. Finally they heard the ship's bell ring midnight, and as silently as possible they crept out of their prison, stopping at the foot of the ladder to get a small can of oil from a locker where the pirates stored equipment. It would keep the pulleys and ropes that lowered the long boat from squeaking.

Up on the deck, they found the night calm with a murmur of wind and a faint hiss of sea along the sides of the ship. The long boat was at the stern. They would have to sneak past the helmsman to get to it. As Jessica had predicted, however, his head was nodding over the spokes of the big wheel with which he steered. Very quietly, the two young prisoners moved from one deep shadow to another. Whenever the sleepy helmsman looked up, they waited until he dozed again. Finally, they reached the long boat itself.

'Hurry,' urged the mermaid.

Jessica quickly oiled the pulleys, through which ran the long boat's lowering ropes. Then she and the mermaid silently began to ease the boat down to the dark water below. When it got there, they would slide down to it, hand-over-hand.

'Good luck,' breathed the mermaid. She grasped a rope and swung outward. Jessica did the same. Down, down they went, slowly but steadily.

Suddenly there was the shattering sound of breaking glass. The mermaid's tail had struck a cabin window as she slid past. A startled growl came from within and a hideous sleepy face appeared. It was none other than the captain.

'Dive for the sea!' cried Jessica. She dropped into the long boat. But the captain was too quick for the mermaid. One rough fist shot out and grabbed her by the neck. 'All hands on deck!' he stormed. 'Prisoners escaping!'

To her horror, Jessica saw her friend hauled back into the ship. Then feet pounded the deck above, the long boat jerked upward, and before Jessica knew it she was once more handcuffed to the mermaid.

Jeering pirates surrounded them.

'Well, mates,' cried the captain. 'What shall we do with them?'

'Hang them from the yard-arm!' snarled one.

'Slice them into pieces and throw them to the seagulls,' yelled another.

A wicked gleam came into the captain's piggy little eyes. 'At sun rise,' he said, 'they can entertain us by dancing on a plank.'

A cheer burst from the pirates. Jessica shrank

against the mermaid. 'Walking the plank' was a favourite pirates' game. Prisoners were tied hand and foot and made to stand on a narrow board held over the water until finally they fell in and drowned.

'We mustn't give up,' whispered the mermaid. 'Your crocodile friend might still come, or when we fall in the water some other mermaids might be swimming nearby to help us.'

Both knew, however, that there was little chance of either happening. Jessica would drown as soon as the mermaid became too tired to keep her afloat. And the mermaid, handcuffed to her, would not be able to swim away from sharks or other dangerous fish and would soon perish too. So they said their prayers and waited.

Soon, a first crack of grey appeared on the horizon. The whole sky lightened and the sun rose up out of the sea, a huge red ball.

The captain grinned evilly. 'Well, my pretties, still no crocodile? Then it's fish feeding time!'

With hoots of laughter, the crew lashed a long plank to the rail so it stuck well out over the water. Jessica's legs were tied tight together with rope.

'We must jump right away,' Jessica whispered, 'and cheat them of their fun.'

'You are right,' agreed the mermaid.

They kissed quickly and were dragged on to the plank.

'Now! Show us how you can dance!' the captain shouted.

The sharp point of his cutlass forced them out over the water. The ship rolled with the waves. Jessica looked down at the sea and for an instant lost courage and struggled to keep her balance. The pirates shrieked with delight.

'Be brave,' exhorted the mermaid.

'Goodbye,' cried Jessica. She braced herself to leap, and then an unexpected shout came from the lookout high up on the main mast.

'Ship ahoy! Dead ahead!'

All heads turned. Not far away, a raft tossed on the waves. It had one small sail and a makeshift cabin and Jessica couldn't believe her eyes at what else she saw. Seated by the steering oar all alone was none other than the dodo bird.

9

It can't be, Jessica thought. But it was indeed the Professor of Books himself, peering through his steel rimmed spectacles at a big dusty dictionary as unconcerned as if he were at the supper table in Hannah's kitchen. How on earth had he come to be there?

There was a roar of rage from the captain. 'Run him down!' he shouted.

For an instant, Jessica and the mermaid were forgotten. Orders were shouted, sails were trimmed and the ship steered directly toward the raft. Jessica could only think of one thing: to save her friend. With all her strength, she threw herself back on board the ship, pulling the mermaid after her. If she could wrestle the wheel from the helmsman for just one second, she might turn the ship away.

But the captain saw her. 'Hold fast!' he snarled, and he raised his terrible cutlass.

What happened then was completely unexpected.

There was a sudden violent shock which stopped the ship dead in the water. Cursing, the captain went flying down the deck to sprawl on to a shouting tangle of pirate crew. Jessica and the mermaid who also fell had hardly got to their own feet when there was a second shock. The ship shuddered and groaned and nearly capsized. Looking over the rail, Jessica saw a big dark form just beneath the surface of the water.

The mermaid also saw it. 'It's a whale!' she exclaimed.

'It isn't,' Jessica contradicted joyfully. 'It's a hippopotamus.'

And then she heard the most unearthly yell ever and saw something she'd never forget. A magnificent figure in battered brass armour was climbing aboard swinging a great two-edged sword. A bright green plume flowed from his visored helmet and a green crocodile head was emblazoned on his shield.

'Noble knights! Brave men at arms,' the helmet shouted to an invisible army behind it. 'Follow me!' And Alfred swarmed down upon the pirates.

An enraged crocodile is a terrible thing. Taken by surprise, pirates scrambled in every direction for safety. Some lost their heads and jumped overboard. Others were bowled over by the unexpected fury of the attack.

The captain, however, was made of tougher stuff. Pulling his pistol from his waistband, he took careful aim. Brass armour was no match for a bullet. One good shot and Alfred would be finished.

But the captain never fired. At the last instant, three dark and ragged shapes came shrieking out of the sky to zoom like deadly arrows straight for his eyes.

The pistol dropped unfired. Beating off the tormenting crows, the captain fell upon Alfred with his cutlass. Other pirates quickly rallied behind him and a hand-to-hand battle to the death began.

It was ten to one. Steel clanged against steel as cutlass met broadsword. Curses tore the air, men screamed and moaned. Sometimes it seemed the pirates would win, sometimes Alfred. But bit by bit, the pirates slowly gave way towards the rail to make a final choice between the crocodile's terrible sword and the sea.

Suddenly, something changed it all. Sword swinging, Alfred came to the open hatchway leading down to Jessica's and the mermaid's cabin prison.

'Alfred!' screamed Jessica. 'Watch out!'

Too late. One moment victory was at hand; the next, their brave rescuer had disappeared. There was a muffled shout, a clattering crash of armour, and silence. Pirates rushed, whooping, to slam down the hatch and lock it. Jessica's heart sank. In minutes she and the mermaid would be back on the plank and what the pirates would do to Alfred was too awful to think of.

She had not reckoned on the worthy Professor of Books, however. Nor had the pirates. Unnoticed, his old-fashioned morning suit and frock coat damp from the sea, the dodo quietly appeared on the prow of the ship. His educated eye quickly saw what was needed. He picked up a fallen cutlass and with one well directed blow severed the rope which held aloft the ship's huge spreading mainsail.

With a rattling hiss, the rope flew through the pulleys at the top of the mast and the sail fell to the deck, smothering the pirates beneath it so all that could be seen of them was bumps and lumps.

'In case anyone thinks he can crawl out,' the dodo announced in his dry voice, 'I shall arrange to have him rolled on by a large herbivorous quadruped of the order Artiodactyla.' He cleared his throat and added, 'In Plain English, that means a hippopotamus.'

His cutlass sliced another rope. The ship's gangway

dropped with a splash to the water and Hannah, dress and apron streaming, heaved up out of the sea.

One of the crows screamed from high on the mast:

> 'She's a big fat Momma,
> And she weighs a ton.
> If she rolls on you,
> It won't be fun.'

Then he and his friends flew off to pester a seagull.

Jessica and the mermaid were enfolded in big damp leathery arms.

'Oh, Hannah,' Jessica said, 'I thought I'd never see you again.'

'And I don't suppose you ever thought you'd see this fellow either,' chuckled Hannah. She took off her dripping-wet sun bonnet and there was the most wonderful sight ever. Gribit sat perched between Hannah's ears as unruffled as if rescuing his mother from pirates happened every day.

'Had trouble getting him to eat for a while,' said Hannah. 'But no child says no to Hannah's plain good food-sense very long. Not even a duck.'

'Gribit, gribit,' Gribit said happily and pecked at one of her ears.

'Oh, Gribit,' said Jessica, and she began to cry just the way any mother would have done.

10

An unhurt but embarrassed Alfred was rescued from below decks, and with Hannah as a threat the pirates were allowed to crawl out from under the sail and were bound hand and foot.

Soon, Jessica heard all about how she and the mermaid were rescued.

When Gribit returned without her, the crocodile went to where she'd been kidnapped and found the pirates' ransom note. He and the dodo immediately decided to try for a rescue. 'Because once you try to make a deal with pirates,' Alfred declared, 'like with a ransom, you're in even worse trouble. They immediately want more.'

'So we built a raft,' Hannah chipped in, 'and followed the ship until the right moment came.'

'We stayed out of sight,' the dodo said, 'but we could always tell where you were by the garbage the pirates threw overboard.'

'Garbage,' said Alfred testily, 'means rubbish.'

All the time, the rescuers had had little to eat. 'And I'm starved,' Hannah said. So that evening she cooked a delicious feast in the ship's galley and they entertained each other with songs and dances and stories.

The pirates were all locked securely below. The next morning they were given water and dry biscuits and set adrift on the raft. There was a favourable wind which the dodo said would soon blow them back on to the beach where Jessica had been kidnapped.

Then the little party set off in the opposite direction, continuing their voyage to Lady Gleam's at the very, *very* End.

The mermaid had decided to join them, for she confessed, 'Whatever the danger, I want to see the poor princess rescued.'

'But what about your family?' Jessica demanded, thinking of her own mother. 'Won't they be terribly worried about you?'

For a moment, an odd half-frightened half-hurt look came into the mermaid's eyes. Then she said quickly, 'No, they won't be worried. They think I'm visiting a cousin.'

Jessica thought her manner strange and unlike her, but with all the work involved in getting the ship under sail, she soon had to think of other things.

While she and the mermaid steered the ship, Alfred and Hannah heaved and pulled at all the necessary ropes. The learned Professor of Books had brought the pirate captain's charts up on deck and, studying the ship's compass, cried out educated orders. Pretty soon they were well on their way.

After an uneventful voyage of several days, they sighted land. They anchored the pirate ship in a little sheltered cove. 'Out of sight of the pirates if they come looking for it,' Alfred declared. 'And we can use it to get back after we rescue the princess.'

Once ashore, bleak landscape greeted them. It was the edge of the great desert they would have to cross and in the middle of which lived the dreaded cyclops, the one-eyed ogre.

It would be impossible to proceed on foot. The sand would be burning hot and they would not be able to carry enough water and food to last them such a distance.

'Pooh!' declared Alfred, snapping his fingers. 'A sand boat will solve the problem.' Using spare masts and planks from the ship and a wheel from the pirates' cannon, he and the dodo immediately set about building a large and sturdy craft that would sail on runners across the sand like an ice boat on a frozen lake. It took several days. During that time they all camped out on the beach, making a tent from the ship's sails.

One night, shortly before they finally set off, something strange happened. Jessica was awakened by Gribit who in a sudden and unexplained fright, dived under her pillow to hide from something. Hearing faint sounds, Jessica got up and looked out into the darkness. A shadow scurried away from the dying embers of their camp fire leaving behind it the smell of mould and damp and the same feeling of evil the old rat woman had brought into Hannah's kitchen with her.

At breakfast, there was sombre speculation. Was it the old rat woman? If so how could she have so quickly crossed the Pirate Sea? And why had her path crossed theirs on such a wild and empty coast?

Then the sun came up, the breeze was favourable and there was no time to lose worrying. With Alfred at the wheel and its deck piled with water barrels and food, the sand ship set sail, carrying the little party of brave adventurers off into the rolling dunes of the terrible desert.

11

At first the trip was idyllic. At least that is what the dodo called it.

'That means the best you could ever imagine,' Hannah told Jessica.

The weather was indeed beautiful, not as hot as they expected and without a cloud in a brilliant blue sky. At night it was pleasantly cool and the stars even bigger and brighter than at sea. The sand boat sailed better than anyone had hoped for and fairly flew over the rolling dunes.

Perhaps that is just what caused the accident. Alfred was so happy with such a success that he began to sail much too fast.

Coming over one especially high dune, the sand boat actually left the ground for a few feet and little Gribit went flying from Jessica's arms. A split second before he was crushed under one of the runners, Alfred snatched him up from the sand. Doing so, he lost control of the boat.

There was a sickening skid, the sand boat landed sideways at the bottom of the dune and did a somersault. Miraculously no one was hurt and the adventurers crawled shaken but safe and sound from under

the twisted wreckage. 'That's what comes from speed!'
Hannah said severely.

Alfred was unabashed. 'Pooh!' he said, snapping his
fingers with his usual grand air. 'We'll have it repaired
in no time.'

It took much longer than he thought. There was a
broken mast to be mended as well as one broken
runner and a badly torn sail. Far worse, was that
they'd lost one of their two barrels of water. It had
burst open and its contents were sucked up by the
sand at once until not even a damp spot remained.

'We'll have to ration what's left,' the dodo said.

Jessica looked at the mermaid's worried face. The
little sea sprite always required the most water because her scales often needed to be dampened to keep
them from drying up. 'Don't worry,' Jessica reassured
her, 'if you are in any danger you can have my share.'

'You'll do no such thing,' the mermaid said.
'Anyway, I'm certain we'll be quite all right.'

But they weren't. Again something happened.

Before they had finished repairing the sand boat,
the sky suddenly darkened, the wind began to moan.
The three crows flying along behind swooped down
babbling and pointing and in a flutter of black feathers
tried to hide under Hannah's apron.

'Shoo! Shoo! You horrid creatures!' the hippopotamus cried.

The dodo cast his expert eye on the sky. 'There's a
sand storm coming,' he said. 'Quickly, dig a trench
and get down inside it.'

It was too late. With a deafening shriek, a great
blast of wind howled through the dunes. Swirling sand
choked and blinded.

Jessica held on to the boat's anchor with one hand
and on to Gribit with the other. She could see nothing

and could hardly breathe. It seemed forever before the storm finally died away and there was silence.

Jessica dug sand from her eyes and looked around. 'Oh, Gribit,' she said.

'Gribit, gribit,' the little duck peeped.

Of their fellow adventurers there was no sign. Even the sand boat had blown away, leaving behind only the heavy anchor to which Jessica had clung.

'They've got to be somewhere,' Jessica said. 'Especially Hannah. How far could the wind have blown her?'

She set off bravely across the dunes and was soon rewarded by her first rescue. It was one of the crows, half his feathers blown off and head-first down a snake hole. She pulled him out, dusted him off, and ignoring his squawks, continued her search.

To her great relief, she next found the dodo. The venerable Professor of Books was stuck high in a dead palm tree at the edge of a dried-up oasis. Somehow, he had managed to hang on to his knapsack of books.

'Come down,' shouted Jessica. But the old bird had his head buried under a wing and couldn't hear.

Since the tree was not very big, Jessica began to shake it, first a little and then harder, until finally the bird tumbled down beak-over-claws to land, legs in the air, in a most undignified position. Jessica helped him to his feet and he thanked her very formally although, she thought, a little grumpily.

She found a second crow over the next dune, wandering about, his hat jammed over his eyes so he couldn't see. She prised the hat off and he flew away with his friend to help search from the air.

They soon winged back. They'd sighted the crocodile. Once again he had fallen, this time to the bottom of a long-abandoned oasis well. He had lost all his armour but still had his sword. Jessica made a rope of the dodo's knapsack straps and his braces, and it was just long enough for Alfred to grab and climb out.

The third crow was found blown into a sheep's skull set on a rock as a warning to travellers of worse desert to come. The screeching bird was freed by a blow of Alfred's sword and immediately launched into raucous poetry.

> 'What kind of a witch
> Would dream in her sleep
> Of blowing this crow
> Through the eye of a sheep!?'

'Shoo!' Jessica cried, the way Hannah always did, and all three crows flew off to perch on what Jessica at first thought was a big round rock protruding up from the sand.

'She's under here,' one shouted, 'your big fat cow, and to get her out, you'll need a plough.'

Sure enough, what they were perched on was Hannah's big bare backside. The hippopotamus had somehow become buried under the sand with only her rear and the top of her head sticking out.

Jessica chased the crows off and kissed her big motherly friend's nose. A silent tear filled one of Hannah's eyes.

'Can't you move?' Jessica asked.

'No chance, child,' Hannah gasped. 'I've tried to for hours.'

'Then we'll dig you out even if it takes all day,' Jessica said stoutly.

'Not necessary,' the dodo intoned. He produced a magnifying glass from his knapsack and held it carefully between the sun and Hannah. The sun's bright rays were concentrated into a tiny burning spot and in seconds smoke began to rise from Hannah's thick hide.

'Stop it,' she cried. 'At once!'

'It's really just a simple form of what on your side you call a cattle prod,' the professor calmly explained to Jessica.

'I'm not cattle, you – you stuffed museum exhibit,' Hannah bellowed. 'Ow . . .!' With a roar and a huge heave she lurched up out of the sand.

Ignoring her enraged threats to pluck every feather from his tail, the dodo put away his magnifying glass and when Jessica covered Hannah with kisses, the big hippo soon forgot her indignation.

Now they were all together again. All but one. Of the poor little mermaid there was no trace. They spent the rest of the day searching and calling for her, to no avail.

Jessica was heartbroken. No sea creature could possibly survive long in the dry burning sand.

'We can't look further,' Alfred said sadly, 'otherwise we will all die out here. At first light we must set off and pray we find an oasis with water.'

They spent a cold and hungry night huddled at the bottom of a dune. Before she fell asleep Jessica found herself wondering about the crow's rhyme: 'What kind of a witch would dream in her sleep . . .?' Could Lady Gleam have been behind the storm? And what had happened to the old rat woman? She could not answer either question.

At dawn, miserable with growing thirst, the adventurers trudged off in the direction the dodo's compass said they should take.

12

By nightfall, and in spite of brave words of encouragement to each other, lack of water began to win out over the little party of adventurers. Their legs felt like lead, their eyes burned, their throats were too parched to speak. They sat atop a huge dune, too tired even to roll to the bottom out of the desert's cold night wind. One by one, the crows who had scouted the dunes from the air came in to settle dejectedly for the night on some old camel bones bleached white by the sun.

Since they had no food, everyone sat in silence each with his or her own thoughts. Hannah pulled at the hem of her now ragged apron and remembered her tidy little cottage by the bubbling brook. The dodo idly turned pages of his dusty dictionary without seeing a word written there. Alfred dug sand with the point of his sword and thought of the poor princess he would probably never now be able to save.

Jessica clutched poor little Gribit who drooped like a wilted flower and knew that they could not last another day. She watched the sun set, a great red ball that sank lower and lower behind a distant dune and thought of her mother and wondered how she was and if she had ever stopped crying over her lost daughter.

She had been staring at the moving figures silhouetted by the sun for some time before she realized she was seeing anything at all. She could hardly believe her eyes.

It couldn't be, she thought. But it was. There were men on camels riding fast in the direction of the adventurers.

'Look!' she said, pointing.

The dodo and Alfred rose slowly to their feet.

'Bedouin!' croaked the Professor of Books. 'Desert arabs.'

'They shall never touch a hair of your head,' said Alfred bravely to Jessica. He placed himself between her and the approaching strangers and found the strength to wave his sword fiercely.

Then the miracle happened. The adventurers heard a familiar musical voice calling, 'Jessica! Everyone! It's me . . .!!'

And to their utter astonishment, they made out the pale form of the little mermaid up on the front of a bedouin's saddle, her dark hair flying, the silvery scales of her fish's tail reflecting the setting sun.

In a minute, a huge grinning bedouin was handing her down to Alfred. There were hugs and tears and kisses for everyone, even the three crows. Bottles of water were produced from saddlebags and while everyone drank they learned what had happened to their sea sprite friend.

Lifted by a violent twister of wind, she'd been carried high across the desert to be dropped, dazed but unhurt, against the very walls of the ogre's fortress itself.

'It's in a beautiful oasis,' she explained, 'with trees and flowers everywhere and a big lake. And the ogre is terribly nice. He never eats meat and he stammers when he talks, he almost never has visitors and his whole palace has been made ready for you.'

The ride to the ogre's fortress was quickly made. Four bedouin attached a huge sled behind their camels and Hannah rode to the ogre's in style while the dodo and Alfred and Jessica all mounted spare camels. Even the three crows got help, perching on the tip of a laughing bedouin's long rifle.

The stars were out when they finally arrived to find the ogre himself waiting in the gateway of his fortress to greet them.

'We-we-wel-c-come, f-f-riends . . .' he stammered. Except for a tuft of red hair above each ear he was shining bald. He wore long robes like his bedouin soldiers except his were trimmed in silver. The buckle of his wide belt was silver, too, as well as the handle of his huge scimitar and most of his front teeth. Wide silver bracelets jingled and jangled on his great hairy forearms and silver rings gleamed from every fat finger.

His smile was so warm and friendly that Jessica soon found herself quite unafraid of his single eye which just as the dodo had said was in the very middle of his forehead.

Within seconds, the whole party was surrounded by smiling bowing servants, and after the ogre invited everyone to dine with him the following evening, they were shown to palatial connecting rooms looking out over the palm trees at the oasis lake.

There, while their clothes were laundered and dried, Hannah was helped into a specially prepared and cooling mud bath to soothe her dried-out skin;

Jessica and Gribit were shown to a silver tub filled with sparkling spring water; and Alfred was led to a shower where a dozen spouts were shaped like egrets, herons and flamingos. The dodo, who never bathed, was gently treated to a soft jet of warm air which blew all the sand out of his feathers and then every feather was gently dusted, dampened and set back in place. The three crows were offered the same thing but instead flew immediately to perch on the highest part of the fortress roof, each with his head under his wing.

Afterwards, they were all served a special dinner. Hannah got a bale of fresh watercress and some pond grass, Jessica enjoyed a huge silver bowl filled with fruit and nuts and delicious candy, Alfred had a platter of big lake trout which had been caught just for him. The dodo had his favourite dish of garden snails and little Gribit had seeds and greens and some live flies.

Shortly before everyone went to bed, there was a knock on their door and a bedouin soldier came in with the most wonderful surprise of all. Alfred's armour had been rescued from all over the desert. The dents had all been hammered out and each piece burnished until it looked like new.

Lying in bed and thinking how close to despair they had been just a few hours earlier, Jessica couldn't help remembering once more her mother always saying how life was full of surprises. Home seemed farther away than ever and Jessica imagined she was there with her mother, hugging her tight and telling her how glad she was her daughter was alive and well.

If I think hard enough, perhaps she'll somehow know I am alive and well, Jessica thought.

She thought very, very hard and soon fell asleep.

13

After a delicious sleep and a restful day wandering about the beautiful oasis, the little party of friends met the ogre for dinner in his huge marble dining room where there were cool splashing fountains and musicians who played softly from behind the ivory latticework of an ornate balcony.

While plates of food of every kind were served by bowing servants and slave girls, the ogre introduced his wife, a mousy little ogress with a shy smile who said never a word.

Then, he introduced his daughter, Attila, who was quite a different story.

Even taller than her father and monstrously fat, she wore a constant ugly scowl. Her one eye had an awful squint, her teeth were yellow and pointed. She had a straggly moustache, double chins and a voice as hoarse as a frog's. On top of all that, Jessica was quite certain she never, never bathed.

Worst of all, she never stopped correcting and nagging her father who seemed to be thoroughly miserable in her presence.

After dinner and some lively entertainment by

jugglers and acrobats, the conversation turned to where the adventurers were going.

'Ah, Lady Gleam,' said the ogre. 'I've heard of her. She's dangerous indeed and I'm glad I'm protected by so many miles of desert.'

'Is the very, *very* End very far from here?' asked Jessica.

'No, my dear. Across my desert and over the mountains. I will have my cavalry escort you all the way if you wish.'

Then he smiled a little shyly and said, 'All of you, of course, except for my dear friend here on my right.'

With that, he nodded cheerfully at Alfred.

'Me?' said Alfred, astonished.

'Yes,' replied the ogre. 'I'm afraid I must ask *you* to remain with me. Oh, don't be frightened. No harm will come to you. In fact, I shall make you my heir.'

'But why?' demanded Jessica, terribly alarmed. 'Why does he have to stay?'

There was a sudden roar from the ogre's hideous daughter. 'Because,' she shouted, her mouth full of food, 'his name is Alfred and Alfred begins with an A.' Then she showed all her yellow teeth in a triumphant smile.

'What does that have to do with anything?' demanded the Professor of Books and he clacked his bill.

'It has to do with ogre law,' the ogre explained sadly. 'In our country a girl child must always marry a man whose name begins with the same letter as hers. Somehow, we managed to find someone for each of Attila's eleven sisters.'

'My sister Avaricious married Arthur,' bellowed the ogre's daughter, 'and my sister Artful hooked Agamemnon, and Antagonistic found Algier, and Abysmal eventually caught Alexander, and Awful

61

snared Asa and all the rest found idiots whose names began with A and now so have I. I have found Alfred!'

'She's been waiting for this day for twenty years,' simpered her mother. 'A's aren't at all easy to find.'

These were the first words she'd spoken all evening. In spite of everything, Jessica almost giggled because when the ogress opened her mouth she revealed she had no teeth at all.

Hannah, up to now, had been silent. She stood up suddenly and put a protective arm around Alfred. 'Since I am Alfred's landlady and since that's the next best thing to being his mother, I am very sorry to say he cannot get married without my permission and that is something I cannot give.'

'And just why not?' demanded the ogre's daughter.

'Because . . .' Hannah began and then stopped. Being polite she didn't want to say, 'because you are revolting'. Not being able to think of anything else, she looked despairingly at the dodo.

'Because,' said the Professor of Books quickly, 'in crocodile law, a crocodile is only allowed to marry another crocodile.'

'Fiddlesticks,' roared the daughter. 'When in ogre land you do as the ogres do. Not stupid crocodiles. That silly looking reptile there marries me next Sunday if we have to drag him to the altar with a fish hook through his nose.'

Then she rose from the table, and followed by a frightened group of her handmaidens, stormed heavily from the room.

'I'm afraid she's right,' the ogre said apologetically to Alfred who looked suitably horrified. 'I'm sorry about this, dear friend, but I cannot break the law. Not when I am king.'

'Nonsense,' said the dodo. 'Since you are the king you are the law and you can do anything you want.'

'The truth is,' Jessica cried hotly, 'that you just want to get rid of your daughter.'

'Well, wouldn't you?' the ogre pleaded. He pushed back his chair and beckoned to his bodyguard. 'And now I must retire. This evening has quite exhausted me.'

'Just a moment,' Alfred said, suddenly leaping up. 'Nobody has asked me yet what I want to do.'

'Of course they haven't,' countered the ogre, 'you have nothing to do with it. You're just the bridegroom.'

'I don't care who I am,' Alfred shot back stoutly, 'I'm not marrying your daughter. Ever!'

The ogre sighed. 'I sympathize, dear friend. I hardly think I'd want to be her husband myself. It's bad enough being her father. But marry she must and her husband you will be, like it or not.' He nodded at his bedouin guards who grinned back evilly. 'Because,' he continued, 'we have a special room downstairs where all the other protesting bridegrooms beginning with A decided to marry my other daughters in a matter of minutes, just as you shall.'

With that, he left the room.

Alfred sat down slowly, scratching his bumpy head with one webby finger.

Jessica ran to throw her arms around him. 'Don't worry, Alfred, we won't let you get married.'

But for the life of her, she couldn't think of how they could prevent it, and when she looked at the mermaid whose deep-green eyes were dark with worry and at the sombre faces of Hannah and the worthy Professor of Books, she knew they couldn't either.

Even the crows who settled on a chandelier were for once serious. One had started a poem.

'She's a big fat ogress,
Twice the size of me,
Whiskers on her upper lip
Like branches on a tree.
She has yellow teeth
And hairy hands and . . .'

But when one of his pals whispered to him to shut up, his voice trailed off with a low squawk.

It was a gloomy group of adventurers who went slowly up to bed.

14

Three days passed and still nobody could think of a way to rescue Alfred from the horrible fate of marrying the ogre's odious daughter, Attila. The desert stretched seemingly forever all around the ogre's fortress and there was nothing from which to make another sand boat. Stealing some of the bedouin camels was out because Hannah could not possibly ride one and would never be able to keep up on foot with the swift and tireless desert beasts. Pleas by Hannah to leave her behind were of course turned down.

It was Gribit who unexpectedly gave Jessica the idea she thought might save her crocodile friend and everyone else with him.

Watching one of his downy little duckling feathers float gently through the air, she felt a tingle of excitement. She turned to Hannah and the mermaid who were looking out of a window at the paradise oasis which by now had become positively hateful to all of them.

'I have an idea,' she exclaimed. She pointed to Gribit's floating feather. 'What does that make you think of?'

When they both looked blank, she answered the question herself. 'Why, a balloon, of course! If we could make one, we could fly over the desert and the ogre could send all the cavalry after us he wished.'

'It would have to be a very big one,' Hannah said doubtfully, 'to carry me.'

'We can make it as big as we want,' Jessica declared, 'and to fill it with hot air to make it rise, we only need to drill a hole in the wall here. Behind it is the chimney that comes up from the stove in the ogre's kitchen.'

Hannah and the mermaid clapped with joy. 'We can make the balloon by sewing together our sheets,' Hannah said.

'Better still,' the mermaid chimed in, 'let's ask the ogre's wife for lots and lots of material for dresses we'll say we want to wear at the wedding ceremony.'

'Silk would be best,' Hannah exclaimed.

Both the dodo and Alfred were at first a little doubtful. But the Professor of Books finally agreed and took charge of the whole operation. 'Any idea is better than no idea,' he pronounced.

Yards and yards of material were ordered from the ogress who was delighted they had decided to attend the wedding. While Hannah and Jessica and the mermaid sewed it furiously together, beginning that very night, Alfred carefully made a hole through the wall and into the chimney with a homemade drill the dodo designed from a curtain rod.

'What will we use for a gondola?' Jessica asked.

'What's a gondola?' the mermaid demanded. 'We don't have such things under the sea.'

'A big basket for all of us to sit in,' replied Jessica.

'We'll make one out of a bed,' declared Alfred and he sent the crows to the ogre's stable to steal camel reins and ropes with which to attach it to the balloon.

For three nights and days nobody got any sleep at all. Hannah's and the mermaid's and Jessica's fingers and eyes ached from sewing. But eventually, the night before the wedding, they finished. A long fat cigar-shaped envelope of silk stretched from one end of their rooms to the other, slowly filling with air piped in from the kitchen chimney which now was extremely hot from roaring fires built to prepare the wedding feast.

They locked the doors. 'Tell anyone who wants to come in that our dresses are a surprise,' said Jessica.

Alfred and the dodo meanwhile loosened bricks and mortar from around the windows. At the last moment, Hannah would push a big enough hole open in the weakened wall to allow the balloon to depart.

By midnight, the balloon was fully inflated and filled the whole suite of rooms. The biggest bed there, with sides made from chairs, had been stocked with food and water and hung down from it on ropes.

'Do you really think it will carry me, too?' Hannah asked doubtfully.

'It will carry us all,' Jessica said. 'The professor figured it all out with arithmetic and algebra and he's never wrong.'

They all got in to see. Sure enough the balloon, which had risen up to the ceiling, didn't drop a centimetre.

An enormous smile lit up Hannah's face and Jessica gave the motherly hippopotamus an extra hug. 'If it hadn't worked,' she declared, loyally, 'we would not have left, not one of us.'

'Now we must get as much rest as possible,' said the mermaid.

The others agreed and everyone settled down for a short nap. Their plan was to wait until midnight when the whole palace was asleep, then burst open the wall and push the balloon out. Before the guards realized they were escaping, they would be gone.

Sometimes, however, the very best plans don't work out the way they're supposed to.

Jessica had sunk into a deep sleep when the worst possible thing happened.

Alfred had one of his dreams and thought he was attacking the castle of a giant. He jumped to his feet, waving his sword just the way he had back in Hannah's kitchen. 'Storm the walls!' he shouted. 'Batter down the gates. Follow me, brave soldiers.'

And the point of his sword ripped a long gash in the balloon.

By the time the others awoke, the room was filled with the hiss of hot air and the balloon was already half-deflated.

15

'Oh, dear,' said the dodo. 'Oh, dear, dear, dear, dear.' He peered over his steel-rimmed spectacles at the balloon which was now nothing more than a long tube of sewed-together silk, draped limply over the bed they'd made into a gondola.

'What shall we do?' cried the mermaid.

There was no answer from Jessica or Hannah who stared horrified at the useless remains of what had been their only means of escape. Or from Alfred who stood with his mouth open, still half-asleep and unable to believe his eyes.

'Courage,' said the Professor of Books, in what for him was a surprisingly gentle voice. 'The darkest hour is always just before dawn.'

'And dawn is still a half a night away,' Hannah said, pulling herself together. 'Which gives us time for sewing.' She began to rummage among her sewing things for a needle and thread. 'Well, come on you two,' she said to Jessica and the mermaid. 'Get busy.'

'Do we have time?' asked the mermaid.

'Time has nothing to do with it,' clacked the dodo. 'The balloon must be reinflated before the wedding starts and that's that.' He turned to Alfred. 'My friend, you and I have thinking to do.' He led Alfred away and soon they were engaged in earnest conversation.

It was the last time Jessica noticed anything much until the rip was finally sewn shut and the balloon began to fill once more.

By then the sun was well up and the palace filled with last minute preparations for the wedding. The mermaid had fallen asleep in a chair, Hannah was keeping the balloon from tearing on anything, Alfred and the dodo were nowhere in sight.

'Where have they gone?' Jessica asked Hannah. 'The wedding will soon begin.'

'I don't know, child,' Hannah said. 'They went off with Alfred's armour and said the moment we hear the wedding march I am to break down the wall and we are to get in the balloon and fly away.'

'But what about them?' Jessica insisted.

'Alfred said they would both be back,' Hannah replied. 'It has something to do with this rope, although I have no idea just what.'

For the first time, Jessica noticed a rope tied to the balloon's gondola. It crossed the floor and hung out of the window. Looking out, she saw it go back inside the palace through another window below.

What she couldn't see, of course, was what it was attached to and so she had no way of knowing it was all part of a most elaborate plan.

Once more using algebra and arithmetic and even geometry, the dodo had figured how long it would take the balloon to inflate enough to carry them all.

'It will be ready at exactly ten A.M. Not completely full, but full enough,' he'd told Alfred. 'And that is precisely when the wedding starts and when you as groom and I as best man must be at the altar awaiting the bride. Oh, dear, oh, dear. Somehow we will have to be in two places at once. To do that we will have to conjure up some extraordinary deception.'

Which in his language meant, plan some real trickery.

Now, only five minutes before the wedding began, he stood nervously in the palace chapel while the room filled up with servants and bodyguards.

Next to him stood Alfred – except that the dodo knew it wasn't Alfred at all. It was a straw dummy wearing Alfred's armour, right down to helmet and shield. Alfred himself, disguised in a burnous as one of the bedouin guards, had helped him set it up and then gone back upstairs to join Hannah, Jessica and the mermaid.

The rope Jessica had seen was tied to the armour because Alfred had insisted that rescuing his armour was just as important as rescuing himself.

'Without my armour,' he'd said, 'how can I ever become a knight?' The dodo had decided arguing was useless.

There was a sudden flurry at the door of the chapel as the ogre's odious daughter appeared with her father.

'There he is, there's my reptile groom,' she shouted pointing to the dummy of Alfred. 'Start the wedding march.'

Musicians immediately obeyed.

'Wait,' she screamed, stopping them. 'Where are his stupid friends with the new dresses they've been making?'

'Royalty is always honoured by going first,' the dodo said, thinking quickly. 'They will come in after you.'

'They'd better,' snarled the ogre's daughter, and

slightly mollified, she started up the aisle on her father's arm, uglier than ever in spite of her wedding gown and veil.

All eyes were on her. Taking advantage of this, the eminent Professor of Books slipped quietly out of the window to climb as quickly up the rope to the rooms above as his venerable age would allow.

'Hurry!' he gasped as he was helped over the window sill. 'Break down the wall while the music is playing and they can't hear it.'

Hannah, a pillow strapped over her head, stepped forward and butted the wall furiously, once, twice, three times. The wall burst out in a great shower of rock and mortar.

'We're off,' cried Alfred. He and the dodo steered the balloon for the hole as Hannah climbed in the gondola with the mermaid and Jessica.

'Wait!' cried Jessica suddenly. 'Where's Gribit?' She had been so busy that now for the first time she noticed he was absent. She leapt from the gondola and ran through the rooms looking for him.

'Hurry,' cried Alfred. A breeze had come up and was pulling the balloon rapidly outside.

'Gribit, Gribit!' Jessica called.

Directly below, the ogre's daughter had finally reached the altar and the dummy dressed in Alfred's armour.

'You slimy snake with legs,' she hissed. 'In another minute you'll find out what it's like to be married to Attila the ogress.'

The ogre's chief steward was acting as minister. She snarled at him. 'As for you, old man, skip all the mumbo jumbo and get right to the point. Do I, Attila, take this overgrown lizard, Alfred, to be my lawful husband? Yes, I do. And does he, Alfred, take me,

Attila, to be his lawful wedded wife?' She turned to the dummy. 'Well, speak up, you miserable reptile.'

The dummy was silent.

Infuriated, the ogre's daughter slapped it on the back nearly knocking it over. 'Well? Answer, you moronic amphibian!'

And out through the visor of the helmet came a familiar sound: 'Gribit, gribit, gribit.'

Tagging after his hero Alfred, Gribit had crawled inside the helmet and fallen asleep. The back slap had awakened him.

'Gribit, gribit?' screamed the ogre's daughter. She yanked open the visor. 'A duck!' she shrieked. 'And a straw dummy! Help! Help! We've been tricked!'

With a roar, her father came across the aisle to see for himself.

Upstairs, meanwhile, Alfred, hanging on to the broken wall with one hand and the gondola with the other, was nearly being pulled apart as the balloon struggled to rise. As Jessica rushed by, he grabbed her. 'Never mind Gribit,' he shouted. 'I'll take care of him.' And he threw her into the gondola.

'Alfred,' cried Hannah. But it was too late. The balloon shot upward, leaving Alfred behind.

At the altar below, the ogre had just snatched poor little Gribit from the helmet when the whole dummy, armour and all, was yanked through the window by the rope tied to the balloon.

Looking out of the window the astonished ogre saw the balloon sweeping out across the desert.

'After them,' he screamed to his guards. 'And don't come back until you have their heads on the ends of your swords!'

With that, and still holding Gribit by the neck, he raced out of the chapel, followed by his horrible daughter, and bounded up the stairs for the palace roof where he could better watch his guards obey his orders.

16

The balloon, pushed along by the breeze, drifted out over the desert, barely clearing the tops of the dunes because there hadn't been time to inflate it all the way. From its gondola the adventurers could see the ogre arrive on his palace roof with Gribit, and for Jessica it was the worst moment ever.

'Duck soup!' the ogre roared. 'Duck soup!'

'Crocodile stew!' shrieked his odious daughter.

In the palace courtyard, meanwhile, the ogre's guards rushed about getting camels and horses saddled up for the pursuit, all the while howling promises to catch up and shoot them down.

Everything seemed lost. Sea salt tears filled the little mermaid's sea-green eyes. Hannah and the dodo were silent. And when the three crows who'd flown after them came to rest on the top of the balloon, their suspicious-looking bottle was once more tucked away out of sight.

No one had reckoned on Alfred. If he was something of a dreamer, and sometimes seemed to do silly things, he was always resourceful and always very brave.

Still disguised as one of the ogre's guards, he

hurried up to the palace roof after the ogre looking for any possible chance to rescue Gribit.

That chance came when once more the ogre held the little duck up and screamed 'Duck soup!' after the now distant balloon.

Alfred drew his burnous close around his face so as not to be recognized. 'Shall I take him straight to the kitchen, sir?' he muttered. And he put both hands around Gribit's trembling little body.

'Right away!' commanded the ogre, letting go of Gribit's neck. 'And tell the cook lots of stuffing.'

'Your wish is my command, my lord,' said Alfred.

'And if you see the alligator,' screamed the ogre's daughter, 'I want him sliced in pieces this big.' She held up a huge hairy thumb and forefinger.

Alfred bowed and turned quickly away. Too quickly. He didn't notice that one of her huge feet was on the hem of his burnous. With a sharp ripping sound, the burnous tore away from his head revealing who he was.

'It's him!' howled the ogre's daughter. 'The reptile!'

In one bound, Alfred reached the palace stairs, clutching Gribit tightly against his yellow waistcoat. There was no time to plan, but he knew he had to do something and very quickly. A howling mob led by the ogre and his daughter poured down the stairs after him. Reaching the bottom, one way led to the palace courtyard, the other into the main hall of the palace itself.

Alfred hardly hesitated. Outside there might be guards but at least he wouldn't be inside any longer.

He ran into the courtyard.

Then his luck began to turn. Almost the first thing he saw were two magnificent camels with silver saddles. They had been prepared for the desert honeymoon the ogre's daughter planned. Nearby, other camels were loaded with the silken tents that would have made the bridal suite.

Without a second thought, Alfred leaped into the saddle of the nearest camel. Thumping his heels, he urged it through the courtyard gates and into the desert beyond. Guards, thinking he was one of them, did nothing until the ogre's daughter burst out of the palace pointing and screaming, 'Stop him!'

'Hang on, Gribit,' Alfred cried.

The chase was on. The ogre's furious cavalry pursued. Up dune and down they went, Alfred never quite sure if he was following the balloon or not because he could only guess which way the wind was blowing it.

Alfred's camel, carrying not just Alfred but also the heavy silver saddle, soon began to tire. Gaining, the cavalry aimed their old fashioned long rifles. Bullets whizzed by Alfred's head. It seemed to him he would never catch up to his friends but finally he saw them only a few dunes ahead, beginning now to gain altitude very slowly.

Lashing his poor beast into a last effort, the crocodile kept just ahead of the cavalry and finally reached the balloon.

'Alfred,' cried Jessica joyously as he thundered up underneath the gondola. And the dodo and Hannah immediately lowered the rope used to rescue his armour.

Alfred stood in the saddle, grabbed the end and held tight. The balloon surged upward with a gust of wind, yanking him after it.

'Pull,' urged Hannah, and Jessica and she and the mermaid began pulling in the rope with all their strength.

It seemed they would never get Alfred there. Below, there were shouts of rage from the bedouin cavalry, trying now to shoot down the balloon. But finally, first Alfred's familiar crocodile nose appeared at the edge of the gondola, then his lumpy head. Moments later, all of him was aboard, yellow waistcoat, blue jeans, wellington boots and scaly crocodile tail.

'Oh, Alfred!' cried Jessica, throwing her arms around him.

But the greatest happiness was yet to come. When all the hugs and kisses were over, Alfred revealed how he could have climbed a rope and still held on to a frightened, wriggling little duckling.

He opened his mouth and there was Gribit, safe and sound, squatting between the rows of his big teeth.

17

The sun beating down on the balloon warmed the air inside it and it soon soared aloft. Miraculously, only one of the bedouin bullets had scored a hit. This was quickly repaired with a small patch and some glue provided by the ever resourceful Hannah and stuck on by the crows.

Several days before, the dodo had made copies of various maps he'd found in the ogre's library. One showed the mountains bordering the terrible desert. Beyond them, the map showed a lake which the Professor of Books was certain had to be the very, *very* End where Lady Gleam lived.

'We must pray the wind stays just the way it is,' he said, 'because at the moment it is blowing us south by southwest and that is exactly right.'

The wind did, and the desert rolled beneath at a good pace. By noon they could see the mountains and before they knew it were rising up the side of them towards the very highest peaks. The scenery below had changed. Desert sand and rocks were replaced by forests of pine and laurel. There were waterfalls and rushing streams. They saw some deer, some rabbits and a squirrel, and one large ferocious animal which looked suspiciously like a wolf.

'Down inside those mountains are gnomes,' said the dodo. 'Miners of rare crystalline carbon.'

'He means diamonds,' said Alfred.

'Are they dangerous?' asked Jessica.

'They mind their own business and never harm anyone,' he replied. 'Or so I have always heard. Few have ever seen them.'

After a lunch of bread and cheese which Hannah had hidden in her apron while lunching with the ogre the day before, they passed between the two highest peaks of the mountains, coming so close to one they could nearly touch the bare rocks of its crest.

'Look!' the mermaid said. 'A nest.'

Sure enough, on a narrow little ledge there was a big nest made of sticks and twigs and dried grass. Three little downy heads peered out of it.

'Quick!' shouted the Professor of Books, clacking his beak furiously. 'A mirror!'

'What for?' asked Jessica as the mermaid handed him one she'd brought from the ogre's palace.

She'd hardly asked the question when there was a frightened outcry from the crows who took off in every direction and two huge eagles came swooping out of the sky, heading straight for the balloon, their sharp talons spread to claw it to shreds.

'It's the mother and father,' Hannah cried. 'They think we're going to hurt their babies.'

Suddenly one of the eagles shrieked and swerved as a bright spot of light blinded him. The dodo, using the mirror, had reflected the sun into its eyes. 'Try your shield, Alfred,' he ordered.

Alfred snatched up his brightly-burnished shield and just in time turned away the second eagle.

80

'Here comes the first one again,' cried Jessica.

The dodo quickly aimed his mirror again but just then the balloon sailed into the shaded side of the mountain peak where there was no sun. Alfred, risking a terrible fall, stood on the side of the gondola and swung his sword but the eagle ducked and before he flew off to rejoin his mate and his babies, his talons raked the side of the balloon. There was a sharp tearing sound, then the now familiar hiss of air escaping.

Slowly at first, but with gathering speed, the balloon began to descend. From its gondola, the little party of adventurers looked up aghast at the three long slashes the eagle had made.

'We're going to crash!' cried Jessica. She looked down hoping to see some sort of opening in the forest. But there were only trees and cliffs.

'Quick!' said Alfred. 'Needle and thread.'

'We could never sew fast enough,' Hannah said.

'How about some clothes pegs,' Jessica suggested. She knew Hannah always carried a few.

But the motherly hippopotamus shook her head. One of the ogre's slave girls had borrowed them and never brought them back.

'We have something just as good!' the dodo exclaimed. 'The crows.'

'The crows?' the mermaid demanded, completely perplexed.

But Jessica understood and clapped her hands. 'Alfred, call them back. Hurry!'

As confused as the mermaid, Alfred nonetheless put two of his webby fingers to his lips and blew a piercing whistle. Once, twice, three times.

Immediately the crows, now quite far off, flew back.

'The eagles have gone and we need you,' said

Jessica. She quickly explained what they had to do. 'And if you don't,' she threatened. 'we shall all die and you'll be left here by yourselves at the mercy of Lady Gleam who can't be far now.'

Then she climbed up on Alfred's shoulders and held the edges of one tear closed. As soon as she did, a crow flew to hold it that way, using his beak as a clothes peg.

Soon, all three tears were shut most of the way with the crows holding on tight and flapping their wings to keep their balance.

The balloon's rapid descent slowed. 'We may not crash now,' said the dodo, 'but we'll land pretty hard just the same so let's hope it will be on something soft.'

Down the side of the mountains they sped and lower and lower, first over forest, then over a vast and steamy swamp. Suddenly, Alfred shouted, 'Look! The Bottomless Lake.'

Sure enough, beyond the swamp, they could see a lake of jet black water with what appeared to be an island in the middle of it.

'It's Lady Gleam's,' cried Jessica.

Nobody had a chance to say more. There was a terrible crashing sound, the balloon spun sideways as it caught on a branch at the top of a giant cypress tree. Once more air hissed out, and this time the balloon collapsed immediately.

'Hang on!' shouted Alfred.

With a sharp crack, the branch broke and the gondola began to fall, slithering and bouncing from one branch to another, until with an enormous splash it landed in the muddy water of the swamp.

18

Alfred, being a crocodile, suffered least from being dunked in oozing muddy swamp water. Hannah, although she never would have been so unladylike as to admit it, actually enjoyed the unexpected bath. Water, of course, came naturally to the mermaid and as for little Gribit, he at once went off in hot pursuit of water spiders and mosquitoes.

Only the dodo and Jessica suffered and then not much because Alfred immediately hauled them both on to a big flat rock where he made a warm and drying fire from Spanish moss and dead branches cut from trees with his sword.

It was soon evening. Some last bread and cheese from Hannah's apron served as supper and when the silken remains of the balloon were cut up, they were able to provide themselves with both blankets and a tent.

'We may be in a swamp and half-lost, and Lady Gleam may be terrible,' Jessica said, 'but I'd rather this than see Alfred married to that awful ogre girl.'

Everyone agreed. They told stories and jokes and wondered about Lady Gleam and what lay ahead.

'How do you plan to rescue the princess?' Jessica asked Alfred.

'I shall first reconnoitre,' answered her crocodile friend.

'That means,' smiled the worthy Professor of Books, glad for once to explain someone else's big word, 'sneak around Lady Gleam's castle and have a close look at it.'

'I need to know how to get in,' Alfred explained. 'And if possible without being seen. Then I must find the prisoner and get her out without anyone knowing. That's always the best way to rescue someone.'

'Will you make another raft?' the mermaid asked.

'I shall swim,' he replied.

'Then I will go with you,' she said.

'No,' Alfred said firmly, shaking his head. 'We don't know what sort of monsters there might be in the lake. You had better stay with the others on shore until I come back.'

The fire had burned low and with the crows roosting in a nearby tree, they all bedded down for the night, which proved uneventful except for the droning of mosquitoes who only bothered Jessica and the mermaid. After being bitten just once, the little sea maiden decided even a swamp was a better place to sleep and promptly dived in. 'Although,' she said, 'I much prefer the salty water of the ocean.'

Jessica pulled her silken covers over her head and didn't stir until she heard Alfred calling and knew it was morning. Hannah was already up and had found a few last crusts of bread and some fruit for breakfast.

'I've discovered something,' the crocodile said later, coming out of the swamp with water gushing from his jeans and waistcoat. 'There's a road over there.' He pointed through swirls of mist. 'It seems to head toward Lady Gleam's lake.'

Jessica and the dodo were ferried to it by Hannah and Alfred. To Jessica's surprise, she saw an ancient causeway which disappeared off into the trees and mist. Made of huge stone blocks set on low arches and wide enough for several people to walk side by side, it was badly decayed and half-covered with moss. Weeds grew in the cracks between every stone and here and there stones would be missing so that care had to be taken not to fall through into the water.

'Before we set off,' the dodo said wisely, 'we must know if it goes in the right direction.' He got out his compass, but to his amazement the needle spun around and around, first one way then another.

'How odd,' he said. 'Perhaps since we are at the very, *very* End, there is no direction any more.'

'Well, we can't just stand here forever,' declared Jessica. 'So I guess we'd better take it.'

The little party of adventurers started out. The mermaid rode on Hannah's shoulders, Jessica clutched Gribit close, the three crows followed not far behind.

In a little while, they noticed that all along and on each side of the causeway, there were stone statues. A few were animals but they mostly were of people of all ages. Some were children, some old women and men. Certain ones were obviously royalty since they were wearing crowns or tiaras.

'I wonder who they're supposed to be,' Jessica asked. 'And why there are so many of them.'

But her friends were just as puzzled as she.

As they marched on, the trees in the swamp became more numerous, nearly shutting out the light. Mist swirled. Strange things slithered through the water and huge bats swooped out of the gloom to attack the crows who, terrified, came to perch on the protection of Alfred's tail.

'We'd better get there soon,' Jessica said. 'Or it will be dark.'

They trudged on and indeed it began to get darker and darker. Everyone had resigned themselves to another miserable night when suddenly the causeway came to a dock and they found themselves at the Bottomless Lake whose cold black waters were as smooth and still as a mirror.

'Look!' the little mermaid said, pointing.

'Lady Gleam's castle,' Alfred said.

Indeed, in the very middle of the lake an ancient and ominous-looking castle rose up from the water, its mossy battlements and sheer walls dominated by a high tower. At the top, one weak light in a narrow barred window added to a chilling impression of something very evil.

'Perhaps you should not try to reconnoitre to-night, dear Alfred,' said Hannah in a frightened voice.

'What's that sound?' Jessica asked. She'd heard what she thought was the creak of oars in rowlocks.

In fact, she was right. A dark funeral barge, draped in black crepe was coming across the lake. Its dozen oarsmen wore black monk-like habits with cowls which hid their faces. As it got closer, everyone smelled the same odour of damp and rot and felt the same cold wind they all remembered being brought to Hannah's cottage by the old rat woman and which had troubled Jessica when they camped by the sea. Looking more closely, they saw the oarsmen were also rats, with red eyes and claws and long tails.

The helmsman called out a greeting. 'Welcome, Alfred and friends. Lady Gleam awaits you.'

'How did she know who we are?' whispered Alfred.

'She's a sorceress, remember?' Jessica said.

'What do we do now?' asked the mermaid and shivered.

'I can cut them to pieces with my sword,' Alfred said, and he grasped the sword's hilt with both webby hands.

'You would hardly rescue the princess by doing so,' snapped the dodo. 'And you would surely put Lady Gleam more on her guard.'

'If we went back up the causeway a little,' Hannah suggested, 'and made another fire, we would perhaps have time to think up some sort of plan.'

Jessica thought that a good idea. She turned to look behind her at the causeway and immediately felt cold fear grasp at her heart.

Except for the dock they were standing on, the causeway had disappeared and in its place there was only the dark muddy water of the swamp with its crowding-in trees shrouded in mist.

19

'It seems we have little choice,' remarked the dodo dryly, clacking his big beak and adjusting his steel-rimmed glasses.

'Just the same,' declared Alfred, 'we must be prepared.' And as the funeral barge slid gently up to the dock, he began to buckle on his armour hurriedly.

He had just put on his shin guards when a sudden and intense flare of light nearly blinded everyone.

Jessica recovered first. What she saw was as astonishing as the disappeared causeway. All of Alfred's armour, including his sword, had vanished.

It was a silent and thoroughly frightened little group of adventurers, even Alfred, who were bowed aboard the barge by the rat helmsman. Now they saw that each rat oarsman wore beneath his monkish robes a steel helmet, a sword and a suit of black chain-mail, a knee-length mesh sweater made from woven strands of steel. They were soldiers. Alfred ground his teeth in silent rage and Jessica stood close to him and squeezed his hand to make him feel better.

In minutes, the black-draped barge had silently skimmed the dark water of the Bottomless Lake and the foreboding walls of the castle loomed over them. A huge iron portcullis lifted and they arrived within the castle itself at a damp stone landing lit by flaming torches stuck in iron wall brackets.

A dozen rat soldiers lined each side of a stair going up to a heavy wooden door, and as they stepped out of the barge they were greeted by none other than the old rat woman herself, dressed in her long skirts, thread-bare sweater and tattered shawl.

'Welcome, my friends,' she simpered, her little red eyes darting from side to side. 'Lady Gleam awaits you.' And she rubbed her paws with their long curved claws together.

The moment they saw her everyone knew they had been tricked into coming there right from the start, although nobody could understand why. Was there really a prisoner princess? Or had the old rat woman been sent with a story about one just to entice them? And if so, why?

They followed the old rat up the stairs between the rows of soldiers and found themselves in a vast torch-lit courtyard crossed back and forth by scurrying servants and soldiers, all rats. Looking up, they saw it was surrounded on three sides by several tiers of long open hallways which could be seen into from below through wide vaulted arches.

In the very centre of the courtyard was the castle donjon, a high round stone tower reached from the top hallway by a narrow bridge to a heavily guarded door about half way up. Far above and just below its roof was the dimly-lit and barred window they had seen from the swamp.

'Lady Gleam lives there,' the old rat woman said, pointing to it. 'She will join you at dinner. Meanwhile, she has asked me to show you to your rooms.'

'Where is the princess?' Alfred demanded.

'The princess?' The old rat's little red eyes glinted. 'Perhaps you should ask Lady Gleam.'

Then beckoning, she started up a wide stair to the first hallway. Jessica and her friends followed and soon found themselves going along the first floor hallway from which, through its open archways, they could now look back down on the courtyard.

At the end of the hallway, they reached a large suite of candlelit rooms, obviously prepared well in advance of their arrival. Fires crackled in big stone fireplaces, great four poster beds were turned down. Flannel nightgowns were laid out for everyone and there were pitchers of steaming hot water for washing.

'I will come back in an hour to escort you to the dining hall,' the old rat woman told them and hurried away.

'Well,' said Jessica, looking around, 'since we seem to be prisoners ourselves, we might as well make the best of it. I shall take a bath and have a nap before she comes back.'

The others agreed and went to their own rooms and an hour later when the old rat woman reappeared, they were all rested and ready to meet their hostess.

'I wonder what she's like,' the mermaid said to Jessica.

'I can't imagine,' replied Jessica, 'since I've never seen a sorceress.'

'She'll wear a high cone-shaped hat and have fingernails as long as claws and have black eyes and snow-white hair,' said Hannah.

Alfred and the dodo thought she'd appear in different forms; a snake one moment, a bat or an owl the next. For, as the Professor of Books explained, sorcerers and sorceresses could change themselves into anything they wanted, whenever they wanted.

As it turned out, they were all to be proved completely wrong.

20

An hour later, the old rat woman returned to lead them back down to the courtyard and across it to the castle's great dining hall. It was so magnificent it took Jessica's breath away. A hundred royal banners, some ancient some new, hung from flagstaffs high above a long marble banquet table set with gold plates and cutlery and with rare crystal glassware. A rat footman in black and gold livery stood at attention behind each chair. The mantelpiece of an enormous fireplace was decked with gold candelabras and three huge crystal and gold chandeliers with a hundred candles each lit up the farthest corners of the high vaulted ceiling.

The table was set for seven, three on each side and one place at the end where the chair was as big and ornate as a throne.

The old rat woman disappeared. A resplendent butler bade the friends be seated. Engraved gold placecards told each where to sit; the mermaid, Alfred and the dodo occupied one side of the table while Gribit, Jessica and Hannah took the other.

They waited expectantly.

'Where is she?' asked the mermaid.

She was answered at once. There was the deep

vibrating sound from somewhere of a large gong and suddenly Lady Gleam was there, as if by magic, at the head of the table.

For a moment the adventurers were so surprised they could only stare, for each found herself or himself looking at a beauty surpassing even the mermaid's.

Lady Gleam was a slender young woman barely out of her teens, with raven black hair that came down just to her shoulders, with skin as white as marble and with lovely sapphire blue eyes. She was dressed in a simple unadorned black evening gown. A large black onyx ring decorated one of her thin tapering fingers and a graceful locket of the same stone hung from a delicate gold chain around her neck.

She looked slowly from one guest to the other and with a warm and engaging smile, sat down.

'Welcome,' she said in a soft and musical voice. 'I am so glad you are all finally here. What extraordinary adventures you have had. You, Jessica, coming down through the whirlpool like that; it was really very brave of you, even if you were saving your child.'

Ignoring Jessica's surprise, she turned to Alfred. 'And you, dear friend, so bravely fighting all those pirates after Hannah smashed into their ship.' She smiled at Hannah. 'I hope you didn't suffer too much headache afterwards. And as for you, worthy Professor of Books, you played your silent role masterfully. I believe your ancestor, the famed mathematician Dodecimal, once did something similar to save a city but that was nearly fifteen hundred years ago so I can't remember precisely.'

Finally she said gently to the mermaid, 'Getting caught like that by those dreadful pirates was silly, but I shan't say more about it for you and I have a secret we want kept, don't we?'

Astonishment, then fear clouded the little mermaid's sea-green eyes. She bit her lip and twisted her fingers.

For an instant no one else could speak, either. How did Lady Gleam know so much about them? And how on earth could she remember the dodo's ancestor, Dodecimal?

As if reading their minds, Lady Gleam laughed lightly and said, 'Oh, I am sure you are wondering how I know so much about you, but as you said yourself, Jessica, while waiting for my barge to bring you here, I am a sorceress and if I choose to know, I can.'

Alfred finally could contain himself no longer. He burst out hotly, 'All right for all that, but where is the princess you hold prisoner?'

'Princess?' Lady Gleam looked surprised then laughed again. 'Ah, yes. It seemed a pity to fool you that way but I needed you so badly I couldn't take the chance of your turning down an ordinary invitation.'

Jessica found her voice. 'Need us? What do you need us for?'

'Not you actually, Jessica,' Lady Gleam said. 'I really only wanted Alfred. I tried to send all the rest of you home with a sandstorm, but it didn't work out right, did it?' She turned to the crocodile. 'You shall soon have the knighthood you've dreamed of so long, my friend, for I am the Queen of Darkness and can knight anyone I please. But you must grant me a favour first.'

'What's that?' demanded Alfred who had at first brightened but then, remembering she was a sorceress, quickly became suspicious.

By way of answer, Lady Gleam waved a slender and beautiful hand at the royal banners hanging overhead.

94

'Each one represents a kingdom I conquered,' she explained. 'Some long ago. Now, the only kingdoms left are so far away it costs too much to send an army to them. So I thought of a different way to keep my treasury full. You, my friend,' she continued 'will go forth to bring me damsels of my choosing from whose fathers we will demand the highest ransoms possible. Any maiden will do as long as her father is really rich, but princesses will be best because most kings will give their whole kingdoms to rescue their daughters.'

While Alfred stared speechless she added for the others, 'As for the rest of you, after some training Jessica will replace my old rat woman who is becoming very careless with age; Hannah can teach my chefs real home cooking and the professor . . ."

She got no further. With a roar of anger, Alfred leapt to his feet and seized a sword from an ancient suit of armour standing by a wall. 'Me? Alfred? Kidnap damsels and hold them for ransom? Never!'

Lady Gleam smiled indulgently. 'I am afraid, my friend, you perhaps have more bravery than brains.'

With that, she turned her onyx locket in the direction of the dodo. A click, the lid flew open revealing a dark mirror inside. The dodo's reflection appeared in it. There was a blaze of light and the Professor of Books instantly vanished.

'Your scholarly friend is now a stone statue on the causeway across the swamp,' Lady Gleam declared, 'like so many others who have chosen to defy me. If you do not go tomorrow, Alfred, in search of our first prisoner, the rest of your friends here will join him there.'

She rose from her throne-like chair. 'And now I

must retire. Enjoy your meal. Someone will show you back to your rooms when you have finished.'

Then, just as quickly and silently as she had appeared, Lady Gleam disappeared again.

21

In spite of everything, when Jessica and her friends went to bed they fell into a deep and exhausted sleep.

Waking to daylight, Jessica quickly dressed and went to look out of her window. She was just in time to see the black-draped funeral barge which had brought them all to the castle heading back towards the swamp. Her heart sank. A familiar figure stood on its deck. It was Alfred setting off to take his first prisoner, his armour tied in a neat bundle beside him.

She heard a sound and turned to see Lady Gleam coming to join her. The young sorceress wore a black cloak and dark blue slippers which matched the sapphire-blue of her eyes. Her smile was warm, her voice soft.

'Good morning, Jessica. I hope you slept well. Your mermaid and hippopotamus friends were up early and are no longer in their rooms.'

'Where is Gribit?' Jessica demanded. She suddenly realized the little duck wasn't there.

'He is having his first singing lesson. We shall see him after I have shown you the castle.'

With that, Jessica found herself being led down one

long draughty corridor after another. They began at the castle's highest battlements where rat soldiers in black chain mail kept constant watch in case intruders dared to cross the lake.

They visited the armoury where rat workers made new weapons; swords, shields, spears and war axes. They saw the library where dusty volumes filled shelves in a jumbled mess.

'They've got into a terrible state over the centuries,' Lady Gleam said. 'Perhaps you will be able to arrange them for me.'

In the kitchens, a dozen cooks prepared food. Among them was Hannah who, to Jessica's horror, was attached to a massive iron stove by a heavy chain locked around one leg.

'Don't fret, child,' the big hippopotamus whispered when Lady Gleam turned her back a moment. 'Just keep your ears and eyes open. Everyone has a weak spot and sooner or later Lady Gleam will reveal hers.'

In the dungeons far below, they found the poor mermaid, locked away in a dark dripping-damp cell whose door was guarded by four heavily-armed soldiers.

When she and Jessica had tearfully embraced, the mermaid turned pleading eyes on Lady Gleam. 'Can't I just swim about in the Bottomless Lake?' she asked. 'Since I can't walk far alone, I could hardly flee over the mountains and across the ogre's desert by myself.'

'You are far too valuable for me to take any chance with,' was the reply. 'Have you never told Jessica who you really are? Perhaps you should unless, of course, you want me to.'

The frightened look Jessica had seen before came

again into the mermaid's sea-green eyes. She hesitated, then confessed tearfully, 'My father is King of the Sea, Jessica.'

'Then you're a princess,' Jessica cried. 'A real one!'

'Yes,' the mermaid admitted. 'We quarrelled and I did something very silly. I ran away from home and got captured. I never told you because I was afraid Alfred would take me back to my father so he could be knighted and then I would be punished.'

'Alfred would never have done so if you had asked him not to,' Jessica told her little friend, 'even though he wants to be knighted more than anything. And as for your being punished if you go home, I am sure your father would be so glad to see you, he'd no longer be in the least angry.'

'Glad enough to pay a fortune for you,' Lady Gleam said in a cold voice. 'And you shall stay in this dungeon, my dear, until you write to your father telling him he must send all the pearls in the sea to me as your ransom.'

'I shall never!' cried the mermaid.

'Then sit and shiver, curse you,' Lady Gleam hissed, and pushing Jessica out of the cell slammed the iron door.

Reluctantly, Jessica followed her captor back upstairs.

'We shall go to my rooms next and you shall see your little Gribit,' Lady Gleam said with a smile. She had instantly regained her composure, but Jessica had seen the real Lady Gleam unmasked and wondered how she and her friends could ever escape from anyone so heartless and evil.

They climbed to the highest hallway above the courtyard and Jessica soon found herself carefully treading the narrow bridge which led to the middle of the donjon.

Soldiers came to attention on each side of the door and they entered the donjon itself. There, a narrow circular stairway dimly lit by the occasional oil lamp spiralled upward around an open void that disappeared down into inky darkness.

'Below,' said Lady Gleam, 'is the Lake. In olden times, they used to throw those they wanted to get rid of forever off the stairs here.'

With a strange smile, she started upwards and more frightened then ever, Jessica followed, staying as far from the edge of the stairs as she could.

They climbed and climbed and finally arrived at the door to Lady Gleam's apartment. The sorceress produced a ring of keys and selected one. The door opened and they entered a big circular room. By a shaft of daylight coming through the one narrow barred window, Jessica saw a heavy four-poster bed draped in black, a fireplace with a freshly lit fire and a table with some books and what seemed to be a large crystal ball. There was also a desk and near it the old rat woman who sat in a straight-backed chair, sewing.

Jessica paid little attention to any of it. Her eyes went at once to a cage hanging from the ceiling. In it sat Gribit, looking quite forlorn.

'Has he sung yet?' she heard Lady Gleam ask the old rat.

'Not a note, your ladyship.'

'He will,' Lady Gleam said. 'And like a nightingale.' She turned to Jessica. 'I put a spell on him, you see.' She nodded in the direction of the window. 'His friends there too.'

Jessica looked and saw two of the three crows

perched on the sill. To her surprise, one had turned bright green, the other bright blue.

'I want them to turn the colour of gold,' Lady Gleam went on. 'But they're stubborn, or perhaps it's because they drink so much, so I shall make them come every day for a new attempt. One refused and has joined your dodo friend on the causeway.'

She approached the table and looked into the crystal ball. 'Ah,' she said, 'our aspiring knight.'

'Alfred?' Jessica ran to look. Sure enough, Alfred appeared, eyes sorrowful and trudging through a deep forest.

'And here is the object of his search,' said Lady Gleam. She tapped the crystal ball and a pretty young maid appeared, admiring herself before a mirror.

But Jessica hardly saw her. She had suddenly remembered something the veritable Professor of Books had found in one of his dusty volumes the night the old rat woman stopped in for soup.

'Lady Gleam eats but once a year,' she'd read, 'and then it's to feast off the heart of a fresh-killed child of royal blood.'

Since she'd learned the mermaid was a real princess, it was quite clear to Jessica what would happen to her once the King of the Sea had paid the ransom Lady Gleam demanded.

22

A week passed. Directed by the old rat woman, Jessica slaved from dawn to dusk, learning to take her place as Lady Gleam's servant. She remembered Hannah's advice that everyone had a weak spot, but as each day went by she grew more and more convinced the sorceress had none.

One of her everyday jobs was to clean up Lady Gleam's workshop, a small cluttered room in an isolated far corner of the castle. The sorceress sometimes spent all night there concocting potions or poisons. Along with ancient books dealing with black magic, alchemy and witchcraft, there were rows and rows of bottles from which she would take such frightening ingredients as powdered bats' wings or ground snails' horns, frogs' livers, spiders' eyes, leaves of deadly nightshade, dried toadstools and other strange herbs.

While Jessica cleaned, the old rat woman would put a kettle on coals that always glowed in a small iron brazier and never went out. She would get down a cup and when the kettle had boiled make some morning tea. Into it she would pour exactly six drops of something from a little gold flask she took from a locked cupboard. Jessica would finish her work and they would take the tea to Lady Gleam in her apartment.

One day, after the old rat woman had prepared the tea, she accidently bumped into Jessica. The cup slipped from her claws and fell to the floor.

'Clumsy girl!' she shrieked. 'Lady Gleam will have us both thrown to the bottom of the donjon. Clean up the mess while I make more.'

When the new tea was ready and she reached for the little gold flask, however, she found only one drop left in it. With muttered curses, she pulled an ancient volume from a shelf of books and shuffled frantically through the pages to find what she wanted. Reading from it, she quickly collected ingredients from various bottles and mixed them together, pausing in her haste only when she saw Jessica watching her.

'Don't stand there gawking, girl,' she snarled, gnashing her long yellow teeth. 'Get about your work.' And she gave Jessica a sharp blow on the ear.

As soon as the mixture was ready, she added precisely six drops to the new tea, poured what was left into the little gold flask and put it back in the cupboard.

Then, locking the work room behind them with a big key from a key ring like Lady Gleam's she hurried Jessica to the donjon.

All the rest of the day Jessica found herself thinking about what she had seen. What was in the little gold flask? Why had the old rat woman been so upset and rushed to make more?

As she was sweeping Lady Gleam's floor, Jessica suddenly remembered the old book the old rat woman used. In her haste, she had forgotten to put it away.

Jessica could hardly contain herself with excitement. If she could get the book, she might discover what it was the sorceress was drinking every day and something told her that could be very important.

But how? Her eyes fell on the two crows sitting on Lady Gleam's window sill. They had come a few minutes before, as they did late every afternoon, to have their colour changed. One was now bright pink, the other purple.

Lady Gleam was busy at her desk. If she heard whispering, heaven only knew what she would do, perhaps turn them all to stone. Jessica thought, then waved her broom at the two unhappy birds.

'Shoo!' she cried. 'Ugly things. You've had your new colour for today. So go somewhere else with your messy feathers. If you must sit on a window sill, you can sit on mine if you promise not to bother me.' And she quickly winked at them.

The two crows flew off. Lady Gleam looked up from her desk and smiled. 'How well you are learning, Jessica. Now come and comb my hair.'

When her work was finally over Jessica ran as fast as she could go back to her own room. To her relief, the two crows had indeed understood her and were perched on her window sill.

'There's an open book in Lady Gleam's workshop,' she told them. 'If you get it, I'll ask Hannah to bring you something special from the wine cellar tomorrow at bedtime when they unchain her.'

The crows flew off. Ten minutes later, covered with soot, they were back with the book. 'The window was shut,' they explained, 'so we flew down the chimney.'

Jessica opened the book at once and saw its dusty pages contained hundreds of formulas for mixing magic potions. There was one to make you invisible and one to give you unheard-of strength. Another would make you sleep for a hundred days and yet another keep you awake for the same amount of time.

Then Jessica came to a page where the book clearly had been opened many times. On it there was a formula to keep you young forever.

'Of course,' Jessica said aloud to herself, because everything was immediately explained. It was why Lady Gleam could talk of her library being neglected for centuries and about conquests of kingdoms a thousand years ago. It explained why some statues on the causeway looked as though they had been there nearly forever and how the sorceress remembered Dodecimal, the dodo's famous ancestor.

Jessica knew she had finally found Lady Gleam's weak spot. The sorceress must be thousands of years old, kept young by the drops poured every day into her tea from the little gold flask.

After reading the formula she was rewarded again. In very small print below it was written the word 'Antidote' and after it another formula. Jessica didn't need anyone to tell her what that word meant. An antidote to any formula was what you gave someone to make the formula not work or to reverse whatever it did.

She turned to the crows who at the prospect of something from the wine cellar had brightened considerably. 'I want you to do one more thing,' she told them, 'and if you succeed, I will see you get twice as much as I promised.'

Then, beckoning to them to come very close and whispering very softly, she told them exactly what they were to do.

23

When Lady Gleam went to bed it had just struck midnight.

The old rat woman picked up her clothes as usual, folded them neatly over a chair, turned out the lights and went out to a lumpy straw mattress at the head of the stair which wound down around the inside of the donjon.

If Lady Gleam needed her during the night, she would pull a golden cord by her bed and a little bell would tinkle near where the old rat slept.

Hanging her long skirt, tattered old sweater and shawl on a peg along with her ring of keys, she pulled a dirty old blanket around her and closed her evil little eyes. Soon, she was asleep.

The moment her snores drifted down the donjon's cold damp stairs, two shadowy shapes flitted through a window to land right next to her.

Jessica had smeared the two crows with chimney soot to hide their bright pink and purple colours and they looked almost as dark as they were supposed to be. Very quietly, one lifted the old rat woman's skirt and sweater from its peg, the other her shawl and key ring. Then both flew out again.

Swooping up over the castle's battlements and towers, they soon were perched on the end of Jessica's bed where, their work done for the moment, they tucked their heads under their wings and promptly fell asleep.

With a shudder, Jessica put on the sweater and pulled the filthy old shawl around her head. Both smelled terribly of rat and the skirt was a little long but that would help because her feet would be hidden.

Then, tucking the old book with the antidote formula under her arm and taking the ring of keys, she left her room.

The castle was in darkness. Wind sighed and moaned through open windows and down empty corridors. As she made her way through it to Lady Gleam's workshop, Jessica stooped over, imitating the old rat woman's shuffling gait.

Twice she stole past dozing guards. But a third one woke up and wanted her to tell him all the latest castle gossip. Jessica's heart nearly stopped with fright. She pulled the shawl close around her face and imitating the old rat woman as best she could, snarled, 'Mind your own business!' and hurried on, expecting at any moment to hear footsteps behind her. To her relief when she dared look back, his head was nodding again.

When she reached the workshop, she locked the door behind her, lit a candle, opened the old book and after timidly shooing away several large flitting bats, set to work at once.

The formula was complicated, calling for many different kinds of powders, herbs and evil-looking liquids which needed to be boiled in a pot over the ever-burning coals of the iron brazier until the sand in an hour glass ran out twice. It seemed forever before she'd found them all, some on one shelf, others on another. It seemed even longer before she had everything measured correctly, checking the book's instructions over and over to make certain she'd made no mistakes.

Minutes ticked by. In an hour she turned the glass so its sand could run back again. The night began to wear thin. Soon, to Jessica's consternation, there were the first faint signs of approaching day. A thread of grey appeared in the black of the horizon over the swamp across the lake and the stars dimmed.

Finally, the sand in the hour glass ran out a second time.

Jessica removed the pot from the coals and taking great care none should spill, she poured all the liquid left into the little gold flask which she had emptied of its youth elixir, and locked the flask back in its cupboard. Then, tidying up, she left the workshop and locked its door behind her.

Making her way back to her own room, she awoke the sleeping crows and shedding the old rat woman's skirt, shawl and sweater sent them along with her keys back to where she slept outside Lady Gleam's door.

The crows were only just in time. The sky was streaked with light now and birds were beginning to twitter. Bats flitted into cracks in the castle's walls or hung for the day by their feet from high rafters under its many roofs. From somewhere, a cock crowed.

The old rat woman stirred in her sleep, sniffling and snorting and yawning. Very quietly, the two crows hung up the skirt, shawl, sweater and keys on the peg where they belonged and flew out again.

Five minutes later, the old rat awoke, put them on and went to wake up Lady Gleam.

24

To Jessica, the morning seemed to last forever. Lady Gleam had awoken in a bad mood because Gribit still would not sing.

'Horrid little barnyard fowl,' she hissed. 'At least open your foolish beak and try.'

But poor little Gribit just sat, his feathers all puffed up. He looked so forlorn Jessica thought her heart would break.

All morning, then, it was do this and do that and no matter how quickly Jessica did it, the sorceress was never satisfied. Although half-scared to death Lady Gleam would somehow find out she'd changed the contents of the little gold flask, Jessica was relieved when it was finally time to go and clean up the workshop.

As she swept and dusted, she watched from the corner of her eye when the hateful old rat woman made the usual tea, then got down the golden flask and poured six drops from it into the tea cup.

'Hurry, lazy girl, we're late,' she snapped, her little red eyes darting and her tail lashing out from under her long skirts.

Jessica quickly put away the cleaning things and

minutes later, they were climbing back up the dark stairs of the donjon to Lady Gleam's apartment.

The two crows had arrived for Lady Gleam's daily attempt to turn them the colour of gold. She had just cast a spell that made one lavender, the other bright green, when Jessica and the old rat woman came in.

Cursing the crows, the sorceress took her tea to the table where she kept her crystal ball. 'Come see, Jessica,' she said, 'your crocodile friend is nearly home.'

Jessica obeyed. Sure enough, there was Alfred coming slowly down the causeway to the dock where a barge awaited. He was leading the young maiden she'd seen looking in the mirror and both seemed miserably unhappy. Indeed, Jessica thought she saw tears in Alfred's eyes.

'Good!' said Lady Gleam. 'I'll prepare a letter to her father and she can copy it in her own hand as soon as she arrives.'

She went to her desk and Jessica began to wonder if she would ever drink her tea. If she didn't, Jessica had no idea what she would do. The thought of mixing up a second antidote was overwhelming.

Just then, however, Lady Gleam finally raised the cup to her lips. A look of surprise came over her.

'What an odd taste it has,' she said to the old rat woman.

'It's the same as I make every day, your ladyship. Exactly the same,' the old rat whined.

Slightly appeased, the sorceress sniffed at the tea, then shrugged and drank it.

Whatever Jessica expected to happen, and she wasn't sure what it would be, it didn't happen right away. Lady Gleam calmly continued with the letter, smiling to herself at the thought of the money it would make her.

Breathless with expectation, Jessica was obliged to return to her cleaning. She was taking ashes from the fire when Lady Gleam coughed and said, 'You're raising too much dust, girl. Be more careful.'

Her voice sounded different from usual and Jessica, turning, saw that she suddenly appeared older. There were lines around her eyes, her waist had thickened slightly and there was a touch of grey amidst the coal black of her hair.

When she stood up to go back to the crystal ball, Gribit noticed and quacked with surprise. The old rat woman, hearing him, looked around and saw the sorceress herself. A shriek of warning hissed through her yellow teeth. She pointed a trembling paw.

In one second, Lady Gleam was at the mirror, saw what had happened and instantly suspected why.

She grabbed up the tea cup and tasted a last drop in it. 'I knew it,' she cried. 'It's not elixir, it must be the antidote.' She turned on the old rat. 'Fool! Someone's tricked you. Make some more elixir quickly. And bring it as fast as you can run.'

With that, she pushed the old rat woman out of the door and turned raging eyes on Jessica. 'Wicked child! You're the only one who could have done this. Very well, you shall join your dodo friend.'

With a chilling laugh, her hand flew to the locket hanging from her neck. The lid snapped open, revealing the dark mirror inside. And she turned it toward Jessica.

That was too much for the two crows. They came to life and screaming, attacked in a flurry of wings and feathers, pecking at Lady Gleam's eyes and trying to tear the locket from her hand.

111

Beating them back, however, she managed to turn the locket on one. He vanished instantly. With a terrified squawk, the other gave up and looped back out of the window to safety.

Their attack, nonetheless, gave Jessica a chance as well as new courage. She threw herself on the sorceress and tore the locket from her neck, hoping to use it on her, but then couldn't get it open again.

Hair white now and shoulders stopped, Lady Gleam fought to get it back. And in spite of her onrushing age which had already begun to weaken her, she nearly succeeded. Screaming curses, she had prised open Jessica's fist, closed tight around the locket, when her head came near to Gribit's cage. Seeing his chance, the little duck pecked hard through the bars.

'Vile creature!' she cried and, infuriated, forgot herself for just an instant and slapped at him.

That instant was all Jessica needed. Taking no chances, she threw the locket out of the window, broke free from Lady Gleam and ran to the door. But one look down the donjon stairs was enough. She could never escape that way. The old rat woman had alerted soldiers and a stream of them were rushing upward, yellow teeth chattering and swords drawn.

Lady Gleam had left her keys on her desk. Jessica hurriedly grabbed them and locked the door, then shut its heavy bolts.

'Break it down!' screamed Lady Gleam, for now she was helpless to stop Jessica herself. In seconds she had become even older, her fingers gnarled, her back bent.

As the rats threw themselves against the door, Jessica shoved her easily to one side and began to pile furniture against it. But she did so with faint heart because she knew it was only a question of time before they broke in and all was lost.

25

The barge carrying Alfred and his prisoner had crossed the Bottomless Lake and had nearly slipped under the castle's portcullis to the landing stage inside its walls, when the last crow came zooming out of the sky like a lavender dart.

And breathlessly he told Alfred everything that had happened.

If Alfred was invincible when attacking the pirates, there is no word to describe what he became when he heard Jessica's life was again in danger. His big friendly crocodile eyes narrowed to dark pinpoints of rage, the tip of his scaly tail quivered. But he remained silent until after the portcullis had closed behind the barge sealing him into the castle.

Then, whispering to his poor prisoner to be brave and go nowhere until he returned, he went into action. Between him and the castle courtyard beyond the damp steps from the landing stage, were a score of deadly rat soldiers. Not bothering to don his armour, Alfred unsheathed his sword and with a roar that must have turned their blood cold, he attacked. The rats went down like ninepins.

Wrenching open the heavy wooden door, he raced

across the courtyard and up the stairs, heading for the bridge to the donjon. Already a swarm of rat soldiers streamed across it to reinforce their comrades trying to enter Lady Gleam's apartment. Sword whistling, Alfred arrived and piled into them, tumbling rats right and left off the bridge to their deaths in the courtyard far below.

High above, Jessica heard the uproar. She looked down, saw Alfred far below and screamed for help.

Because she did, something like an explosion occurred down in the steamy kitchens. There was a speaking tube between there and Lady Gleam's apartment over which the sorceress gave orders to the head cook. It carried Jessica's scream to the hippopotamus and it was all it took to fire Hannah's protective instincts.

'Jessica!' With a bellow twice as loud as Alfred's roar and oblivious to the huge stove to which her leg was chained, the big hippopotamus headed up the kitchen stairs to the courtyard, dragging the stove behind her.

In a far corner of the castle, meanwhile, the old rat woman hastily finished making some new youth elixir. Clutching the little golden flask, she hurried from the workshop without even bothering to close the door.

She arrived at the bridge to the donjon, ducked around a swarm of rat soldiers retreating before Alfred's sword and started up the donjon's long winding stair.

In Lady Gleam's apartment, Jessica had by now piled everything she could find against the door. But under attack by the rat soldiers, it had begun to splinter and give way. First sword points appeared, then holes big enough for long-clawed rat paws to push through.

Even more terrifying were the hideous chattering

screams from the rats of what they would do to her when they finally got in.

Lady Gleam was now a helpless ancient crone half her former size. Her back was bent double, long hairs sprouted from her chin and nose, her hands were like the rats' claws. A horrid smell of dank mustiness and rot came from her shrivelled body. And when she shouted at Jessica, 'Wicked child, you will never see your mother again!' her voice was nothing more than a whispered croak.

So odious was she, in fact, that Jessica tried to stay as far as possible from her, praying the old rat woman would get there too late with fresh elixir.

But the old rat woman had finally reached the top of the stairs and was just the other side of the splintering door. 'Hurry! Hurry!' she screamed at the soldiers who had now opened up a hole in the door almost big enough for her to squeeze through.

That was when Alfred finally arrived, cutting a path through the rats and spilling them by the dozen off the stair and down into the inky darkness far below. He saw the old rat woman start to slip through the hole in the door, he saw the small golden flask in her paw. He didn't know what it all meant, except he knew it had to be bad.

'Stop!' he commanded and swung his sword.

Too late! The sword sliced through only the old woman's tail, leaving it to writhe about on the stone landing like a nasty brown snake.

Then, from Lady Gleam's apartment, he heard Jessica scream again. 'Alfred! Hurry!' In a new fury, he attacked the door himself, trying to get through it to her.

He didn't have to bother. One ton of enraged hippopotamus mother had finally arrived. She came up the last step of the stair still dragging the huge coal-spewing iron stove behind her, and without pausing an instant for breath, smashed through the door as though it were matchwood.

'Jessica!' Hannah bellowed. 'Jessica!'

And the good dear laundress lady, oblivious to Alfred, to the old rat woman, to Lady Gleam or to anything, ploughed across the apartment, scattering broken furniture left and right and holding out great leathery brown arms to Jessica who threw herself into them.

Alfred, following, spotted the old rat woman and dived for her.

With a squeak of terror, she ducked and rushed out of the door on to the landing. One of her paws stepped on a hot coal from the stove. It was like stepping on a burning golf ball. Her hind feet went out from under her, she screamed and shot off the landing to plunge down the donjon's dark shaft to the black waters of the Bottomless Lake far, far below.

When Alfred turned back to Jessica and Hannah, he found them both staring wide-eyed at a little mound of dry powder in the middle of the floor.

It was all that was left of Lady Gleam.

As they watched, there was a sudden chill draught of wind. The powder swirled around and around and in a dark spiralling eddy, vanished out of the open window.

26

Hot coals from the stove Hannah dragged behind her set the castle on fire.

There was no time to lose. One of Lady Gleam's keys set the big hippopotamus free, and with Jessica holding Gribit close the adventurers hurried out of the donjon, down through the smoke and flame to the dungeon where they freed the poor little mermaid from the darkness of her damp cell.

With Lady Gleam gone forever, an extraordinary thing happened. All her rat soldiers and servants immediately turned into ordinary rodents, scurrying around on four feet without clothes, chain-mail armour or swords, and so terrified of the fire that they paid no attention at all to anybody.

Alfred led Hannah, Jessica and the mermaid up from the dungeons to the courtyard and to the black-draped funeral barge that had brought them to the castle. When he had raised the portcullis, each took an oar and they started back across the Bottomless Lake.

They were just in time. The castle was now a huge torch of flame. Everywhere rats were swimming for their lives.

Halfway across the lake, the mermaid suddenly exclaimed, 'Look!'

They all turned just as the castle, with a deep hissing roar, fell in upon itself. A last column of flame lightened the evening, then it sank slowly into the lake whose dark waters closed over it.

Now, a new and amazing sight greeted the adventurers. On the dock and the causeway, hundreds of people of all ages milled about in confusion. Lady Gleam's stone statues had come back to life.

To the joy of the little party on the funeral barge, one was their dear friend, the Professor of Books, who clutched his dictionary and looked about as though nothing had happened to him.

Above, three ragged shapes soared and tumbled and cartwheeled, enjoying themselves for the first time in weeks. One had what was clearly a bottle from Lady Gleam's wine cellar and he shouted down in a raucous voice:

> 'Lady Gleam's been sent to hell.
> Her castle's sunk,
> We're freed from her spell.
> All that's happened
> Is just a bad dream,
> Gone up in smoke and
> A cloud of steam . . .'

That night, although nobody had much to eat or drink, there was a happy celebration as all those freed from being stone made plans to return to their own lands and kingdoms.

'But how on earth will we ever get back to Hannah's Haven?' Jessica asked, thinking of the mountains and the ogre.

'The Bottomless Lake,' Alfred replied, 'flows into a

river and the river goes around the mountains and the desert and eventually into the Pirate Sea.'

'Eventually means after a while,' the dodo explained. 'Or finally,' he added, clacking his bill.

Jessica laughed. 'We'll take all that horrid black cloth off the barge and maybe we can find some plants in the swamp which will have a dye we can use to change its colour.'

They did, and two days later headed down the river in a barge now turned bright blue.

The trip to the Pirate Sea proved long but uneventful. The weather was sunny and warm. Everyone relaxed and recovered from their dreadful experience. Arriving, they found the pirate ship just where they had left it, anchored out of sight in the little cove at the edge of the desert. Without delay, they set sail.

All this time Jessica and Hannah kept secret from Alfred the fact that the little mermaid was a real princess. The mermaid had promised to return to her father and ask him to knight Alfred, but in case something went wrong they didn't want their crocodile friend to be once more disappointed in his dream.

One morning after several days at sea, the mermaid told Jessica they were at her home. Jessica asked a puzzled Alfred to stop the ship and when he'd done so, the mermaid went to the bow and began to sing quietly.

Presently, a voice answered her. To the adventurers' delight, another mermaid appeared, then another and another, until there was a score of them laughing and playing all around the ship and calling to the mermaid to join them, which she quickly did.

'Her father should appear at any moment,' Jessica announced.

'Her father?' Alfred said, not understanding.

Jessica had no time to answer. The mermaids had formed a circle in the water, holding hands, and in the middle of that circle suddenly appeared a large merman. He had long green-grey hair and a green-grey beard and wore a magnificent crown of sea shells inlaid with gold. In one hand he carried a gold sceptre. It was the King of the Sea himself. With a warm and loving smile, he took his daughter in his arms.

It was then Jessica finally told Alfred who the mermaid really was and how his greatest dream in life was finally about to come true.

'By tonight, dear friend,' she said, putting her arms around him, 'you will no longer be an aspiring knight, but truly Sir Alfred the Great.'

There was no reply from Alfred whose heart was too full and who simply stared and stared at the King of the Sea and his little daughter.

But Jessica didn't need an answer. The smile on her friend's face and the tears of joy in his eyes, were worth every minute of trouble they'd all been through on their long adventure to rescue a princess from Lady Gleam.

27

The ceremony of knighthood was magnificent and beautiful.

Towards the end as Alfred knelt before the King of the Sea to be touched on each shoulder with a golden sword and while a chorus of lovely mermaids sang softly, Jessica thought of her mother.

Suddenly, no matter how much she loved all her new friends, she wanted more than anything to go home. By the time they had said a tearful goodbye to the little mermaid, promising to meet her again soon, it was almost all she could think of. Gribit had grown up. He was suddenly a young drake with a pretty blue-green head, a silver grey chest and with blue and white tips to his dark wing feathers. He had nothing more to fear from little cousin Hokey and there was no reason now for her to stay on 'this side' any longer.

Reaching the beach where she had been captured by the pirates, they scuttled the ship so the pirates could never use it again and went ashore. After all their adventures, the walk through the forest to Hannah's Haven seemed nothing at all and before she knew it, Jessica found herself once again sleeping under the thatched roof of the cozy cottage by the brook.

At breakfast the next morning, she was trying to find a way to tell Hannah how she felt without hurting her feelings when Hannah suddenly said, 'Jessica, I think you ought to go home to your real mother. It's not fair to her to stay here any longer. Besides, you're skipping too much school.' She eyed Gribit. 'He'll miss you when you go north but you could leave him here, if you wish, where he has his friend Alfred. We'd be glad to have him and he'd always remind us of you.'

So that morning, Jessica went to the brook with all her friends and waited for the whirlpool to begin. The three crows sat on the bridge, once again passing back and forth a most suspicious bottle. One shouted noisily,

> 'Back up through the whirlpool,
> Off to school,
> Stuff your head full of knowledge
> And end up a fool.'

Then all three fell about laughing like maniacs until Alfred threw a clod of earth at them and told them sternly to be quiet.

The whirlpool began to turn slowly and make its strange moaning sound.

Jessica gave the worthy Professor of Books a hug and a kiss on his big clacky beak. 'I shall always think of your multifarious knowledge,' she said, 'and you can look up that word yourself.'

For Hannah, there were tears as she was nearly smothered in a huge leathery-armed motherly hug. 'I love you, dear Hannah, and I will come back, I promise.'

She turned next to the crocodile who had put on all his armour for the occasion except his plumed helmet which he carried under one arm. Taking his webby hand, she curtsied gracefully to him and took out her handkerchief.

'Sir Alfred,' she said, 'I give you this to wear on your sleeve forever as my champion of champions and as an expression of my love for you.' Then she kissed him gently on top of his nobbly head.

The whirlpool had started to turn faster and faster. Jessica scooped up Gribit. 'Gribit,' she said. 'Oh, Gribit!'

She began to cry. How could she possibly leave him and perhaps never see him again? But she at once realized she was being silly. Real mother-love was to want what was best for your child, not for yourself, and Gribit would have a lovely life at Hannah's Haven.

Jessica gave him a last hug and put him down.

'Go now,' Alfred urged. 'The water's just right.'

Indeed, the whirlpool was turning at full speed.

'Goodbye,' cried Jessica. 'I'll be back.'

And she dived in, head first.

Once again, as long ago, she was beaten and buffeted about as though by huge wet pillows. Just when she thought she could stand it no longer, she found herself sitting on the edge of the dark pool of water in the swamp where it had all begun.

'Golly!' exclaimed Jessica aloud. She stood up and looked down the narrow path which led out of the swamp to her cousin Andrew's back yard. There, sure enough, was cousin Mary-Lou watching little Hokey in his play pool.

Jessica found herself running. 'Cousin Mary-Lou,' she cried. 'It's me! Jessica. It's me!'

Sometime later when cousin Mary-Lou and cousin Andrew had recovered from their overjoyed surprise, when Jessica had telephoned her mother to say, 'It really *is* me and I'm well and coming home on the bus tomorrow,' Jessica remembered something very important she had to do.

It was night-time. Everyone was asleep. She stole from bed and out into the back yard. There, very quietly, so as not to arouse the other ducks or any of the chickens, she scooped up a pretty little girl mallard and, holding it close, took it into the swamp to the whirlpool.

There was a moon whose soft light filtered down through Spanish moss hanging from cypress trees and turned the night swamp mist into silver. She waited until the dark water began to turn and moan.

'Nobody believed a word I told them about the "other side",' she said to the little duck, 'or about Alfred and Lady Gleam. They all thought I'd been kidnapped or had amnesia or something. Amnesia means you lose your memory. So you're the only one who will ever know it's true.'

The whirlpool was turning rapidly now, so with that she tossed the little duck into its swirling waters and it disappeared in a flash on its way down to Gribit.

Fiction in paperback from Dragon Books

Ann Jungman
Vlad the Drac   95p ☐

Thomas Meehan
Annie   £1.25 ☐

Michael Denton
Eggbox Brontosaurus   85p ☐

Marika Hanbury Tenison
The Princess and the Unicorn   £1.25 ☐

Alan Davidson
A Friend Like Annabel   £1.25 ☐
Just Like Annabel   £1.25 ☐

T R Burch
Ben and Blackbeard   £1.25 ☐
Ben on Cole's Hill   £1.25 ☐

Jonathan Rumbold
The Adventures of Niko   £1.25 ☐

Marcus Crouch
The Ivory City   95p ☐

Lynne Reid Banks
The Indian in the Cupboard   £1.50 ☐
I, Houdini   £1.25 ☐

Nina Beachcroft
The Wishing People   £1.25 ☐
Well Met by Witchlight   £1.25 ☐
Under the Enchanter   £1.25 ☐
A Visit to Folly Castle   £1.25 ☐
A Spell of Sleep   £1.25 ☐
Cold Christmas   £1.25 ☐

Carol Adorjan
The Catsitter Mystery   £1.25 ☐

To order direct from the publisher just tick the titles you want
and fill in the order form.

Fiction in paperback from Dragon Books

Richard Dubleman
The Adventures of Holly Hobbie   £1.25 ☐

Anne Digby
Trebizon series
First Term at Trebizon   £1.25 ☐
Second Term at Trebizon   95p ☐
Summer Term at Trebizon   £1.25 ☐
Boy Trouble at Trebizon   £1.25 ☐
More Trouble at Trebizon   £1.25 ☐
The Tennis Term at Trebizon   £1.25 ☐
Summer Camp at Trebizon   £1.25 ☐
Into the Fourth at Trebizon   £1.25 ☐
The Hockey Term at Trebizon   £1.25 ☐
The Big Swim of the Summer   60p ☐
Me, Jill Robinson and the Television Quiz   £1.25 ☐
Me, Jill Robinson and the Seaside Mystery   £1.25 ☐

Elyne Mitchell
Silver Brumby's Kingdom   85p ☐
Silver Brumbies of the South   75p ☐
Silver Brumby   85p ☐
Silver Brumby's Daughter   85p ☐
Silver Brumby Whirlwind   50p ☐
Son of the Whirlwind   65p ☐
Moon Filly   60p ☐

Mary O'Hara
My Friend Flicka Part One   85p ☐
My Friend Flicka Part Two   85p ☐

To order direct from the publisher just tick the titles you want
and fill in the order form.

Fiction in paperback from Dragon Books

Peter Glidewell
Schoolgirl Chums | £1.25 ☐
St Ursula's in Danger | £1.25 ☐

Gerald Frow
Young Sherlock: The Mystery of the Manor House | 95p ☐

Frank Richards
Billy Bunter of Greyfriars School | £1.25 ☐
Billy Bunter's Double | £1.25 ☐
Billy Bunter Comes for Christmas | £1.25 ☐
Billy Bunter Does His Best | £1.25 ☐
Billy Bunter's Benefit | £1.25 ☐
Billy Bunter's Postal Order | £1.25 ☐

T R Burch
The Mercury Cup | £1.25 ☐

Granville Wilson
War of the Computers | 85p ☐

Marlene Fanta Shyer
My Brother the Thief | 95p ☐

David Rees
Exeter Blitz | £1.50 ☐

Anne Knowles
The Stirrup and the Ground | £1.25 ☐

Erik Haugaard
Chase Me, Catch Nobody | £1.25 ☐

Joan Lowery Nixon
The Spectre | £1.25 ☐
The Séance | £1.25 ☐

Caroline Akrill
Eventer's Dream | £1.50 ☐
A Hoof in the Door | £1.50 ☐
Ticket to Ride | £1.50 ☐

Michel Parry (ed)
Superheroes | £1.25 ☐

To order direct from the publisher just tick the titles you want
and fill in the order form.

All these books are available at your local bookshop or newsagent, or can be ordered direct from the publisher.

To order direct from the publishers just tick the titles you want and fill in the form below.

Name _____

Address _____

_____

Send to:
Dragon Cash Sales
PO Box 11, Falmouth, Cornwall TR10 9EN.

Please enclose remittance to the value of the cover price plus:

UK 45p for the first book, 20p for the second book plus 14p per copy for each additional book ordered to a maximum charge of £1.63.

BFPO and Eire 45p for the first book, 20p for the second book plus 14p per copy for the next 7 books, thereafter 8p per book.

Overseas 75p for the first book and 21p for each additional book.

Dragon Books reserve the right to show new retail prices on covers, which may differ from those previously advertised in the text or elsewhere.